VIRTUALLY
PERFECT

DAN GUTMAN

Hyperion Paperbacks for Children

New York

Dedicated to Adam Trotta

First Hyperion Paperback edition, 1999
Revised Hyperion Paperback edition, 2003

1 3 5 7 9 10 8 6 4 2
Printed in the United States of America

Library of Congress Cataloging-in-Publication Data
Gutman, Dan
Virtually perfect / Dan Gutman.
        p.   cm.
Summary: When twelve-year-old Yip uses his father's new
software to make a computer simulation of a boy his age, the
creation breaks out of cyberspace into the real world and
begins to complicate Yip's life.
ISBN 0-7868-0394-0 (trade)—ISBN 0-7868-2344-5 (lib.)
ISBN 0-7868-1745-3 (pbk.)
[1. Computers—Fiction. 2. Science fiction.] I. Title.
PZ7.G9846Vi 1998   97-34849
[Fic]—DC21   CIP   AC

Visit www.hyperionchildrensbooks.com

Contents

INTRODUCTION

I always loved to build stuff.

When I was still in a crib, Mom told me, I was already making statues with Duplo blocks. As I got older, I graduated to Legos, Tinkertoys, Lincoln Logs, K'nex, Construx, and an erector set. Any time a new toy came out that let you build something, I wanted it.

I built houses out of playing cards. Statues out of toothpicks. Army forts out of wooden blocks.

And then one day I built something that was so amazing, so incredible, that I may never build anything again. That's what this story is about.

—Lucas "Yip" Turner

CHAPTER 1

The Emergency

When I opened the front door that afternoon, I didn't immediately sense anything wrong. It had been a long day at school. I was beat. I just wanted to grab a snack and veg out in front of the tube for a while before tackling my homework. My parents were still at work and my sister wasn't home yet. I wasn't sure where Grandpa Leo was.

"Yip," a low voice groaned when I stepped into the front hall. "Yip!"

My real name is Lucas Turner, but at home everybody calls me "Yip." You see, my dad and Grandpa Leo have always been in the movie business. Dad named me Lucas in honor of George Lucas, but Grandpa wanted me to be called Willis, like my dad. Willis O'Brien was the guy who created the ape for the original *King Kong* back in 1933. Grandpa idolized him. But Dad always hated being named Willis, and he refused to name me Willis, Jr.

It was my mom who settled the dispute by nicknaming me "Yip." Yip Harburg was the guy who wrote the words to the songs in *The Wizard of Oz*. That's her favorite movie.

"Yip . . . " the voice pleaded.

I almost stepped on a big red wet footprint on the tile floor of the hallway. Ketchup? Paint? *Blood*? Quickly, I followed the footsteps toward the kitchen.

Grandpa Leo was lying there, facedown. There was blood smeared on the floor all around him. My cat, Freddy, was sniffing him. A long knife handle stuck out of Grandpa's back, just below the shoulder blades.

I was rocked. I almost didn't notice Grandpa's hand. It was detached, on the floor a few feet away from the rest of him.

"Ahhhhhhhhhhhh!"

I didn't try to scream. It just came out of my throat involuntarily. Freddy yowled and dashed out of the kitchen.

"Yip . . . it hurts. . . . "

"Grandpa!"

I reached for the wall phone to dial 911. I punched in the "9" and was about to punch in the first "1" when Grandpa Leo suddenly leaped up off the floor and grabbed the phone out of my hands.

"Stop!" Grandpa shouted. "What are ya tryin' to do, Yip? Get us in trouble? Nine-one-one is only for *emergencies*!"

Then Grandpa broke up laughing.

CHAPTER 2

A Different World

I should have known. The bloody footprints. The knife in the back. The severed hand. It was so obvious!

"I had you there, didn't I?" Grandpa Leo chuckled.

"Yeah, you got me, Grandpa," I admitted. "You scared me to death."

Before he retired, Grandpa was an F/X guy. In the movie business, F/X stands for "special effects." The F/X guys are responsible for making spaceships, monsters, bullet wounds, fires, explosions, and other fake stuff look real.

Grandpa was an F/X guy for over forty years, and he knows every trick in the book. He used to work on monster movies, science fiction films, horror flicks, stuff like that.

"Yank that knife out of my back, will ya, Yip?"

I pulled at the knife, but it was stuck in there pretty good. Grandpa had hammered it into a block of wood, and strapped the wood to his back to make it look as though he had been stabbed. He cut a hole in the back of his shirt for the knife to stick out.

"They gave me this hand when we finished shooting *Attack of the Puppet People* in 1958," he said, admiring the bloody hand as I jiggled the knife back and forth. "I knew it would come in handy some day. Hey, get it? *Handy*?"

"Grandpa, you need a hobby," I grunted. The knife finally slid out of the wood. I almost fell backward pulling it out.

"This *is* my hobby," he replied, as he started mopping up the fake blood off the floor. "It's all I ever wanted to do."

My sister Paige breezed in the front door. She's fifteen and can be a jerk at times, but she's usually okay. Paige looked around the kitchen. She saw the blood, the knife, and the severed hand.

"Grandpa," she said calmly. "You need a girlfriend."

"Your grandmother was the only girl for me."

Paige and I looked at each other. Grandma died so long ago I don't remember her at all and Paige barely remembers what she looked like. We all think it's about time Grandpa Leo started dating again. My folks have tried to fix him up with women his age, but he always says they're stupid. Or boring. Or old. Or ugly. Or *something*.

"They only want me for my money," Grandpa Leo likes to say. But Paige told me Grandpa doesn't *have* any money. That's why he moved in with us recently.

I feel kind of sorry for Grandpa Leo. It's not just because he's lonely. Movies used to be his whole life, and since he retired he doesn't even go see them anymore. He mostly sits around watching tapes of the movies he worked on back in the 1950s and 1960s.

Freddy finally peeked his furry head into the kitchen to nuzzle Grandpa. Freddy's full name is Federico Feliney. Grandpa named him after his favorite movie director, Federico Fellini.

"Ta ta, boys!" Paige chirped, as she dropped her books onto the kitchen counter. She grabbed an apple, stroked Freddy, and flitted out the door. We only moved into town a month ago, but Paige is already real popular at school (unlike me). She's always running to work on the yearbook or paint scenery for a play or something.

When we had cleaned up the mess, Grandpa asked me what I was planning to do that afternoon.

"Nothin'," I replied.

"You must be doing *something*."

"Watch some tube, maybe."

"Haven't met many friends yet?"

"Not really," I replied.

"What about that boy Joe Kursweil you brought home?"

"He takes karate after school. He's a jerk, anyway."

"Why don't *you* take karate?"

"Karate's stupid."

"How about that kid with the red hair? Why don't you invite him over again?"

"Pete Sahut. He takes piano lessons. Another jerk."

"Everybody's a jerk, huh?" Grandpa asked.

I guess Grandpa Leo felt sorry for me, because he asked if I wanted to do something with him. "That is, if you don't mind playing with a seventy-five-year-old coot," he added.

"I don't mind, Grandpa," I said. "Wanna play some *Sudden Death Football*?"

"What's that?"

"A computer game," I told him. "It's really cool."

"I have a better idea," Grandpa said. "Let's go to the playground and toss a *real* football around."

"I can't throw a football very well."

"You'd get better if you'd play less computer football and more *real* football."

"I don't even *have* a football, Grandpa."

"I'll *buy* you one," he replied. "You know, nothing on a two-dimensional screen is *ever* going to be as much fun as throwing a ball back and forth. Nothing! Didn't your dad ever show you how to throw a ball?"

"No," I said. "But you should see the graphics in *Sudden Death Football*, Grandpa! They're awesome!"

"Are they better than the graphics *outside*?" he asked, pointing out the window. "Why *simulate* reality when you can *have* reality, Yip? It's right outside the door! It's free! You don't have to install it on your hard disk drive. It won't crash on you. And it's user-friendly!"

Reluctantly, I agreed to take a walk to the playground at Jefferson Park with Grandpa. He took a basketball out of the garage and bounced it as we walked. Grandpa seemed all excited, saying he hadn't been to a playground in years.

I used to live in Los Angeles. Grandpa did, too, in his own apartment. Now he lives with my family in the town of Sunnyvale, in northern California. It's about halfway between San Jose and Palo Alto in Santa Clara County, a little south of San Francisco. You may have heard of the area referred to as "Silicon Valley." A whole bunch of big high-tech companies—Apple, Hewlett-Packard, Xerox, and a lot more—are located within a few miles of my house.

As we walked to the playground, Grandpa Leo told me this part of the country was all farmland years ago. They grew oranges, artichokes, garlic, and pumpkins in the Valley.

Then U.S. Highway 101 and Route 237 stretched across the Valley and around San Francisco. All those computer companies moved in and the farmers left one by one. Today, Sunnyvale is mostly boxy office buildings, apartments, malls, and houses like ours. It's hard to imagine that anyone used to grow crops here.

When we got to the field behind the playground, it was deserted.

"Where are all the kids?" Grandpa Leo asked. "It looks like a bomb went off here."

"Maybe everybody's home playing *Sudden Death Football*," I volunteered.

"Where are the seesaws?" he asked, looking all around. "Where are the monkey bars?"

"They ripped them out," I explained. "I heard that a bunch of kids fell off and got hurt. Some of their parents sued the town."

"In my day, the streets and playgrounds were always *filled* with kids," Grandpa said. "Playing ball. Hopscotch. Skipping rope. Don't kids *play* anymore?"

I tried to explain to Grandpa that in most families these days both parents have to work. So most kids are enrolled in after-school programs, classes, and organized sports leagues. The rest of us are home watching TV or videos, or are plugged into the Internet. Besides, it's not safe anymore for kids to play outside without adult supervision. Grandpa Leo didn't really get it.

"No wonder you have no friends," he said.

"It's a different world, Grandpa, that's all."

CHAPTER 3

Don't Try This at Home

"I have an idea," Grandpa Leo said when we got back home. "Let's make a movie!"

I got my dad's camcorder. Grandpa went down to the basement and came out with a big duffel bag and a wooden chair. We hauled everything out to the backyard.

"How about we film a fight scene?" Grandpa suggested. "I'll be the bad guy and you chase me around. You can punch me and stab me and shoot me and stuff."

"Cool."

While I set up the camcorder on a tripod, Grandpa fussed with some props that he pulled out of the duffel bag.

"Okay, you got that camera ready?" he said. "Roll 'em!"

"But we don't have a script or anything," I protested.

"You think we had a script when we shot *Radar Men from the Moon*?" Grandpa asked. "We'll just make it up as we go along."

I found him in the viewfinder, pushed the RECORD

button, and dashed in front of the camcorder.

"Welllllll," Grandpa sneered. "It's about *time* ya showed up, Sheriff. Black Bart don't like bein' kept waitin'. I always knew you was yella. Now I'm a gonna hafta *kill* ya!"

Grandpa's a ham. I think he always wished he could have been an actor instead of working on special effects. Whenever we shoot home movies, he always hams it up.

"Oh, yeah?" I ad-libbed. "How are you planning on killing me, Bart?"

"With *this*." Grandpa reached under his shirt and pulled a revolver out of the waistband of his pants. He pointed it at my head. "Say yo' prayers, Sheriff!"

Grandpa hadn't given me a weapon. I didn't know what else to do, so I rushed toward him. I grabbed the hand with the gun in it and pushed it up in the air.

"Your career in crime is over, Bart!" I yelled as dramatically as possible. "I'm bringing you in."

"You and what army, punk?" Grandpa shouted.

Bang!

The gun exploded a few inches from my head.

"Grandpa! Are you crazy?" I yelled. "That gun is loaded!"

"It's only blanks," he whispered. "Just play along.

Now punch me in the jaw."

I pretended to punch him, and he rolled his head away expertly so my hand just missed. Then he fell backward, letting the gun sail across the yard when he hit the ground. He jumped up quickly and grabbed the wooden chair he'd brought out from the basement.

"You're pretty spunky, Sheriff!" he said. "Well, *this* oughta take some of the fight out of ya."

He raised the chair up and slammed it over my head. I put my hands up and braced myself for the impact, but it never came. I barely felt a thing. The chair shattered into pieces that went flying all over.

"Now grab one of those bottles and whack me with it," he whispered.

I grabbed a bottle. It felt lighter than a regular bottle, so I figured it was safe to smash it over Grandpa's head. The bottle shattered and Grandpa staggered backward, dazed.

"You asked for it, Sheriff," he said, pulling a knife out of his back pocket and waving it in front of my face menacingly. "And now you're a gonna get it. No more Mr. Nice Guy. Now it's time for you to *die*!"

At that moment, our cat, Freddy, wandered out of the house and ran over to Grandpa. He started purring and rubbing himself against Grandpa's ankle. Grandpa pretended it was all part of the scene. He picked up Freddy and held the knife to his throat.

"Don't move, Sheriff," he warned me. "You take one more step, and I cut the cat!"

"You are despicable!" I shouted. "Using a poor, defenseless animal to further your sick plans."

Freddy doesn't particularly like being picked up, and he started wriggling to get free. He jumped out of Grandpa's arms and scampered away.

Grandpa advanced toward me with the knife. I tried to back out of the way as he slashed at me, but Grandpa was too fast. He ran the knife along my arm. A line of blood trickled down, following the path of the blade. There was an evil grin on Grandpa's face.

"Blood!" I said, horrified. "You cut me, Grandpa!"

"Okay, now you're *really* mad. Grab the gun and shoot me right in the gut."

I retrieved the gun from the grass and pointed it at him.

"Any last words, Bart?" I asked.

"Yeah. If I go down, I'm a-takin' you with me, Sheriff!"

He charged me again, and I pulled the trigger. The gun exploded with a force that knocked me backward.

Grandpa flinched. A red blotch appeared on his shirt, and blood started to spurt out of it.

"Ya . . . got . . . me . . . Sheriff," Grandpa groaned,

clutching his belly.

He started stumbling around the grass. Always within camera range, of course.

"I told you . . . they'd never . . . bring me in . . . alive," Grandpa grunted. Then he fell to his knees. "I guess . . . this is . . . the end . . . of the line!" he moaned. "I didn't mean . . . to hurt you . . . Mommy!"

"Will you die already?" I said. "I'm running out of tape."

Finally, Grandpa rolled his eyes up and toppled face-first to the grass with a thud. I blew the smoke from the tip of the gun and turned to face the camera.

"Kids," I said. "We're professionals. Don't try this at home. Let that serve as a lesson to you. If only Black Bart had worked for goodness and niceness instead of badness and evil."

"Cut!" Grandpa shouted. "That was beautiful!"

I was about to turn the camcorder off when a siren screamed down the street. Three police cars skidded to a stop outside our house. A bunch of cops ran out. They charged into the backyard and toward me. They all carried guns, and they pointed them at me, just like they do with bad guys in the movies.

"Freeze, kid!" one of them shouted. "Drop the gun! Put your hands over your head! Now!"

I dropped the gun.

"There's been a misunderstanding, Officer—" Grandpa shouted, getting up off the ground.

"Who's the old guy?"

"He's my grandpa Leo," I told the policemen.

Grandpa dusted the dirt off his pants and walked toward them.

"I'm sorry, Officers," he said. "My name is Leo Turner."

"Were you two yankin' our chains?" one of the cops said angrily as he put away his gun.

"We were just making a little movie," Grandpa explained. "We didn't call the police."

"One of your neighbors dialed nine-one-one."

Suddenly Mrs. Harrison, the old lady next door, came running out of her house.

"Leo! Leo!" she shouted. "Thank goodness you're *alive*!" Mrs. Harrison ran over to Grandpa and wrapped her arms around him like a long-lost relative.

"Oh, stop making such a scene, Liddy," Grandpa said, pushing her off him. "Yip and I were just fooling around."

"You the lady who dialed nine-one-one?" asked one of the cops.

"I heard Lucas scream from the house about an hour ago!" explained Mrs. Harrison. "Then I saw him and

Leo fighting in the backyard. There was a gunshot, a chair, a bottle, *blood*! Leo was holding a knife to the cat's throat! I thought he had finally lost his mind."

Grandpa chuckled, pleased with himself for fooling me, Mrs. Harrison, and even the policemen. He showed the officers his breakaway chair, which was made from balsa wood. He handed them the knife, explaining how he could squeeze its handle and make fake blood spurt out the tip when he moved the knife along skin.

"Corn syrup and red food coloring," he revealed. "Oldest trick in the book."

"What about the blood on your shirt?" one of the officers asked.

"It's a blood bag," Grandpa explained. "I put fake blood in a small plastic bag, attached it to this metal shield, and taped it under my shirt. On the shield is a tiny explosive called a 'bullet hit.' When my grandson fired the gun, I set it off. It exploded the bag and blew a small hole in my shirt. That's where the blood spurted out."

"What are you, mister, a pro?" one of the cops asked.

"Used to be," Grandpa said. "I'm retired now."

"We're gonna let you slide this time, Mr. Turner," the cop said. "But maybe you ought to think about taking up gardening or stamp collecting or something a little more relaxing. You scared this lady half to death."

"I'm sorry, Officer," Grandpa said solemnly. "It won't happen again."

"See that it doesn't," one of the other cops said. "While we were wasting our time here, there could have been a *real* emergency where somebody needed our help."

As the police cars pulled away, Grandpa started giggling and poking me in the ribs with his elbow.

"Did you see the looks on their faces when they came at you with their guns?" he chortled. "Was that great, or what?"

"Did you see the look on *my* face when they came at me with their guns?" I laughed.

Mrs. Harrison didn't think it was funny at all.

"Leo," she scolded, "why don't you act your age?"

"Okay," Grandpa said cheerily. He lay down on the grass, closed his eyes, and stuck out his tongue. "Most people my age are dead."

"Very funny, Leo," Mrs. Harrison said as she stalked back to her house.

"Hey, Liddy, get a sense of humor!" Grandpa called to her. Then he whispered to me, "What a sourpuss!"

Mrs. Harrison slammed her door behind her.

"Boy, I miss making movies," Grandpa said when he'd finished laughing. I fiddled with the camcorder and Grandpa began packing up his props.

"What was the first movie you saw?" I asked.

"It was my eighth birthday," he recalled. "March second, 1933. My dad said he had a surprise for me, and he took me to Radio City Music Hall in New York City. It was the opening night of *King Kong*. I was terrified, but I couldn't tear my eyes off the screen. I knew right then that I would spend the rest of my life in the movie business."

"Is that why you moved to California?"

"As soon as I was old enough," he nodded. "I got a job in L.A. making monsters for RKO Pictures. You know how they made King Kong, Yip?"

"A guy inside an ape suit?" I guessed.

"Nah. That ape was just an eighteen-inch model with sponge rubber muscles and rabbit fur. They shot the model one frame at a time. You see, they'd take a still picture of Kong. Then they'd move the model a fraction of an inch and take another one. And do it again and again. Then, when they ran the film at normal speed, it looked like Kong was moving. It's called stop motion animation."

"Why did you retire from the movies, Grandpa?"

"I didn't retire from the movies," he said bitterly. "The movies retired me. I turned seventy in 1995. That was the year *Toy Story* came out. Then came *Twister* and *Independence Day*. The movie studios didn't need anybody to make monsters or model spaceships or fake gunshots anymore. They could simulate everything on computers. The studios shut down their F/X departments. Nobody wanted old fogies like me around anymore. They wanted kids who could *program*."

He said the word "program" like it was a bad food or something.

"Why didn't you learn how to use a computer?" I asked. "You could have kept working."

"Staring at a screen all day ain't for me," Grandpa said. "I need to build props, handle fire, work with chemicals and electricity. You know, I wired up fifty rocket ships when we made *I Married a Monster from Outer Space*. And then we blew all of them up in five seconds."

"Cool."

"In my day, we used ingenuity. We didn't just move *pixels* around. Whatever they are."

"Pixels are picture elements," I explained. "Every dot on the screen is a pixel. It's probably easier to move pixels around than it is to wire up fifty spaceships."

"Sure it's easier," Grandpa said. "That's the problem. Computers make everything too easy. Instead of learning to spell, you get a spelling checker. Instead of learning to draw, you get a drawing program. Instead of learning to play piano, you get some silly keyboard that plays music *for* you. Instead of sitting down and working hard to learn anything, you just buy a disk. It makes people lazy."

"Yeah, but Grandpa, you have to admit they do incredible simulations on computer. I should take you to a virtual reality arcade."

"Virtual reality!" he snorted. "You mean standing in one place moving your thumb while you pretend you're doing something exciting? I'd rather *do* something exciting, thank you very much!"

"It *is* exciting!"

I knew Grandpa wasn't exactly computer literate, but I never realized what a 'phobe he was.

"Yip," Grandpa went on, "imagine you were born into virtual reality. Imagine you lived there all your life. Everything you ever experienced was a simulation. And then one day some genius discovered this incredible new thing—reality! For the first time, you could actually throw a real ball—not a computer-simulated ball—a *real* ball. And you could catch it in your hand. Wouldn't reality be awesome? Wouldn't it be an improvement over virtual reality?"

"I guess so," I replied. Actually, the idea of living in virtual reality sounded kind of cool to me.

"So why play computer football," asked Grandpa,

"when you can go outside and play real football?"

"Because nobody's outside!" I exclaimed. "Everybody's inside playing computer games."

"Maybe I'm living in the past," Grandpa said, shaking his head. "But honestly, Yip. I think the past was better."

CHAPTER 4

Synthespian

I could tell Dad was angry by the look on his face when he walked in the front door. He works really hard, and he doesn't like coming home to problems.

"Mrs. Harrison called me at work, Pop," he told Grandpa Leo. "I can't believe you were shooting off guns and playing with knives in the backyard."

"*Fake* knives, Willis," Grandpa explained. "Guns that shoot blanks."

"It's still a gun, Pop! Mrs. Harrison freaked out! She thought Yip shot you."

"That old biddy Liddy needs to lighten up," chuckled Grandpa. "We were just having some fun."

I tried not to snicker, but it was impossible. Fortunately, Paige blew in and, as usual, commanded everyone's attention.

"Everybody, I'm in *love*!" she declared, hugging herself.

"Who is he this time?" Mom asked wearily as she zapped something in the microwave.

"He's so cute, Mom," Paige gushed. "His name is David Levine and he's the editor of the yearbook. He said he loved my artwork and he might use some of it."

"That's great, sweetie," Mom said.

It was hard for any of us to get too worked up over this new love of Paige's life. She falls in love with a new boy just about every week. After a while I get tired of hearing about them because I know a week later she'll have completely forgotten about the boy. So why pay attention in the first place?

"How's the movie coming, Willis?" Mom asked Dad as we took our seats around the dining room table. Dad works for Digital Dreammaker, one of the big special effects companies in Silicon Valley. Grandpa helped him get his first job in the movie business—Dad was a gofer for George Lucas on the set of *Star Wars*.

If you don't know what a gofer is, it's somebody who is assigned to go for coffee. Go for sandwiches. Go for whatever the important people need. Dad gradually worked his way up, and now he's in charge of the special effects for *Jurassic Park V: Revenge of Tyrannosaurus*. He's got gofers working for him.

"The movie's going great," Dad said, scooping a hunk of mashed potatoes onto his plate. "We finally finished the scene where the T-Rex steals some nuclear warheads and blows up Mount Rushmore. The explosions are incredible."

Grandpa snorted.

"Cool," I said.

"How did you shoot Mount Rushmore?" Mom asked. "With miniatures?" Mom teaches second grade, but she's learned a lot about special effects from Dad and Grandpa.

"Nah," Dad said. "We just scanned in some photos of the mountain and fiddled around with them until it looked right. You can simulate anything on the computer."

"I know one thing you can't simulate," Grandpa said, his mouth full of food.

"What's that, Pop?"

"A human being," Grandpa replied. "It's easy to simulate a dinosaur. Nobody has ever seen a live one. We don't know exactly how they moved or the sounds they made. Simulating a person would be a lot harder. You can't draw each hair on a person's head. Or the folds in our clothing as we move. Or our mannerisms. I won't live to see the day you create a fake human being on a computer."

"That's where you're wrong, Pop," Dad said. "That day is already here."

Dad doesn't get excited very often, but I could tell he was charged up. He put his fork down and stopped eating. He made big gestures with his hands as he spoke.

"For years, every F/X company has been trying to

build a realistic, lifelike, convincing simulated person. A virtual actor. A vactor, we call it. Well, we finally got the new software today. It's called *Synthespian*. Y'know, synthetic thespian?"

"What's a thespian, Dad?" I asked.

"An actor or actress," he replied. "We only have a beta version of the software, so there may be a few bugs in the program. But the guys in development told me it delivers the goods. I'll start working with it as soon as we finish the movie next week. I can't wait."

"A vactor, huh?" Grandpa said. "And what can a vactor do that a real actor can't?"

"Jump off a cliff without getting killed, for one thing," Dad replied. "We won't have to expose stuntmen to dangerous situations if we can simulate a stunt on the computer. We will be able to create a vactor and stretch him, shrink him, duplicate him, and morph him into any shape we want. We'll be able to chop off his head, put it back on, and use him again for a dozen sequels."

"Awesome!" I exclaimed.

"The best part is, a vactor won't demand ten million bucks in salary. He won't show up late, or show up drunk. She won't throw a fit because her trailer is too small or her boyfriend left her."

"So now they're putting actors out of work, too, eh?"

Grandpa said bitterly. "Pretty soon they won't need cameramen or directors either. Movies will be made by a bunch of hackers sitting at their computers."

"It's already happening, Pop," Dad said. "It's revenge of the nerds. Computers can do magic."

"That's not magic," countered Grandpa. "What we did in *my* day was magic."

"Here we go again," Dad groaned.

"Did you kids ever see *Jason and the Argonauts*?" Grandpa asked Paige and me.

"The movie with the sword-fighting skeletons?" Paige asked. "You showed us the tape a million times, Grandpa."

"*That* was magic!" Grandpa exclaimed. "We blew people's minds with that movie! They had no idea how we made those skeletons dance around waving swords. Today, people look at your dad's special effects and yawn. They know it's all done with computers. They're not amazed anymore. In my day, we told stories using special effects. Now you just blow things up."

"Stories?" Dad laughed. "Yeah, right, Pop. *Santa Claus Conquers the Martians* was a great story!"

"How *did* you make those skeletons fight?" I asked Grandpa.

"Stop motion animation," Dad said before Grandpa had the chance to answer. "That trick is a hundred years old.

You know, the good old days are over, Pop. You were able to do great stuff with what you had back then. You'd put an old sock over an eggbeater and make it look like a tornado. But today, I've got to compete with big screen TVs, surround sound, and interactive multimedia. We need to create special effects that will get people off their couches and into the theaters. We're creating incredible effects. Maybe you should go to a movie for a change and see for yourself."

I didn't want to look. When Dad and Grandpa start arguing about whether or not movies were better in "the good old days," it usually ends with one of them storming upstairs.

"Maybe instead of creating virtual actors on your computer you ought to spend some quality time with real people," Grandpa said. "Yip comes home after school and he has nothing to do. He's got nobody to play with, no place to go."

"Hey, I spend more time with Yip than you spent with me, Pop," Dad said. "When I was a kid, you spent all your time fooling with your fake guns and knives and breakaway chairs."

"I asked you to join me," Grandpa said defensively. "We could have played together."

"I didn't want to play with your props!" Dad shouted. "It's not right to force a kid to play games *you* want to play. You should play what the kid wants to play."

"All you wanted to do was play with your computer," Grandpa retorted. "Yip, did you know your dad was the original computer nerd? When the first computers came out, he begged and pleaded until I got him one."

"Do you still have that PC, Dad?" I asked. "I bet it's an antique. It could be worth a lot of money today."

"No," Dad grumbled. "Grandpa threw it away one day when he was cleaning out the basement."

"It was a piece of junk," Grandpa said. "Then, twenty years later, computers took over special effects. Hackers like Willis became hotshot F/X guys, and I was out on my behind. What a world."

"You were at the top of your craft," Dad said. "You didn't have to retire. You could have kept up with the technology. You were afraid of it. I could teach you how to use the computer in a week. I could even get you a job in movies again if you wanted one."

"I'm not learning how to use any stupid computer," Grandpa said.

"You're just afraid, that's your problem! Computers do everything now. It's time you got used to it."

"Boys," Mom said. "Let's everybody calm down. I baked cookies for dessert."

Mom makes the best chocolate chip cookies this side of Mrs. Fields. She uses them to stop arguments all the time. Given the chance, they could probably stop a war. But not this time.

"I'm going upstairs," Grandpa said, scraping his chair back.

"This place is a bummer," Paige said, clearing off her plate and grabbing a cookie. "I'm going to the mall."

"Can you pick something up for me at Macy's, sweetie?"

"Mom," Paige moaned. "I'm going to hang out with my friends, not to shop."

"Why don't you take Yip with you?"

"Yip doesn't have any friends."

Mom shot a mean look at Paige, then looked at me, I guess to see if my feelings were hurt.

But I wasn't thinking about what Paige said. I was thinking about what Dad said. *A virtual actor.* A vactor. For the first time, it was possible to create a simulated person—out of a bunch of electrons! You could build any person you wanted, to your own specifications.

This could be better than Legos. Better than Tinkertoys, Lincoln Logs, K'nex, Construx, or an erector set.

My mind was racing.

CHAPTER 5

Victor the Vactor

After dinner, I rushed through my homework. Grandpa's door was closed when I walked by. He usually goes to bed early. When I came downstairs, Mom and Dad were asleep in the living room with the TV on. I tiptoed past them and went down to the basement.

That's where Dad keeps his Silicon Graphics Z2000 workstation. It's a supercomputer that's small enough to fit on a desktop. The monitor is huge—twenty-six inches. The Z2000 has more memory than you would know what to do with. The graphics, animation, and sound capabilities are incredible. They need that kind of computer to create special effects for the movies.

The Z2000 costs something like a hundred thousand dollars. Regular people don't have them, of course. But Dad got one through Digital Dreammakers so he can do some of his work at night and on weekends. Sometimes he sits down with me and shows me the cool stuff it can do.

I booted up the Z2000 and waited while the modem initialized itself. The computer is connected into the Digital Dreammakers local area network through a fiber-optic cable. So the data zips along in the form of laser-light pulses through a glass wire that's thinner than a human hair.

WELCOME TO DREAMNET, the screen read after the modem made the connection. ENTER YOUR EMPLOYEE PASSWORD FOR FUTHER ACCESS.

I typed Dad's password and moused around the screen. There was an icon labeled SOFTWARE LIBRARY. I double-clicked it. A long list of programs appeared in alphabetical order. I scrolled down the list until I got to *S* and there it was—SYNTHESPIAN. I double-clicked it.

There were a bunch of options:

- LEARN ABOUT SYNTHESPIAN
- HOW TO GET STARTED
- CREATING A VACTOR
- EDITING A VACTOR
- SAVING A VACTOR

I clicked CREATING A VACTOR.

The program looked as though it worked pretty much like the drawing program I use in computer class at school. Most of the screen was white, and there was a box of drawing tools and a color palette on the left side. When you want to use a tool, you just click on it. Then you can drag it into the middle of the screen and draw or paint with it.

One of the tools looked like a stick figure. That seemed like a good place to start, so I clicked on it. A simple figure appeared on the screen. It wasn't male or female or anything. It had no distinguishing characteristics.

A box appeared that asked, WIRE FRAME? I clicked YES. The stick figure expanded so that it looked more like a human shape, in three dimensions. The entire body consisted of crisscrossing lines, as if the figure's skin was a grid.

MALE OR FEMALE? asked the computer.

I clicked MALE and the character's shoulders grew broader, his arms thicker, and his body a little more boxy. The computer then prompted me to enter the character's height and weight. I typed in 5'4" and 95 pounds, which is my height and weight. As soon as I hit RETURN, the character reshaped itself to the appropriate body shape. It looked something like me, but as a wire frame.

A box labeled SURFACE TEXTURE appeared, with a list of about a dozen options: CHROME, CLOTH, FLESH, LIQUID, METALLIC, WOOD, and others. I clicked CHROME and the wire frame figure suddenly appeared to be smooth, shiny, and silver. It looked like this cyborg I once saw in a movie called *Terminator 2*.

It was pretty cool, but I wanted my figure to look like a person. I clicked UNDO and switched to FLESH. There were several choices, and I selected CAUCASIAN.

My character was starting to look a little human.

There was a menu at the top of the screen labeled ANIMATE. I clicked on it and pulled it down to reveal all kinds of options. It was possible to make the character walk, run, jump, dance, or move any way a human can.

I fooled around with the animate function a bit, then moused over to the menu marked APPAREL LIBRARY. There must have been a thousand little pictures of shirts, shoes, hats, pants, and other stuff to wear. I clicked on some baggy shorts, a T-shirt, and high-top sneakers, then dragged them across the screen. When I placed the clothing over my figure, the computer automatically put the clothing on him.

My figure was looking really human except for one thing. His face. He didn't have one.

I clicked the zoom tool and centered my figure's head in the middle of the screen. Once again, the computer offered hundreds of options in its FACIAL LIBRARY. I clicked and dragged all different eyes, noses, mouths, and chins onto the face.

It was fun to see what my character looked like with just one eye in the middle of his head, or with an ear where his nose was supposed to be. Finally I selected some nice facial features and put them in the right places.

Another menu was marked EXPRESSION. When I clicked HAPPY, SAD, ANGRY, or SURPISED, the face on the screen made that expression.

My character looked pretty lifelike now. He looked like an average kid who moved like a real person. I figured I was just about done, but suddenly another box popped up on the screen.

INTELLIGENCE? YES? NO?

Dad was right. This program really is powerful, I marvelled.

I thought it over. If I was a special effects guy, and I just needed a character to jump off a cliff or something, the character wouldn't need intelligence. In fact, it would be better if he didn't have a brain in his head, come to think of it.

But I wanted my character to be smart. I clicked YES. A clock appeared on the screen, indicating the computer needed time to do something.

After about a minute, a long list appeared on the left side of the screen. It was a bunch of book titles. There were dictionaries and encyclopedias. Almanacs.

Nonfiction books. Novels. Telephone books and comic books and diet books. *The Complete Works of William Shakespeare*. It had everything from Plato and Aristotle to *Miss Manners' Guide to Excruciatingly Correct Behavior*. It was like I had dialed into a complete on-line library.

On the right side of the screen was a graphic of a brain. By clicking on a book title and dragging it over to the brain, I could put that information into my character's database.

I still had a ton of memory left, so I figured I might as well stuff as much information into my character as would fit. I'd make him a real genius. Each book took about a second to download, and after selecting a few books I realized I could take entire chunks of the library at once and download them together.

I selected lots of books, leaving out silly things like *Thin Thighs in 30 Days*. I still had some memory left over, so I added a few joke books like *The Best of Henny Youngman*. I figured my character should have a sense of humor.

The last chunk of book titles was downloading when I heard footsteps coming down the basement stairs. It was Paige.

"I thought you went to the mall with your friends," I said.

"The guys there were jerks, so we left," she replied.

"Whatcha doing?"

"Nothin'."

"It's pretty late to be doing nothing. Mom and Dad already went up to bed."

Paige walked around behind me to see what was on the screen. It was the image of my character running in place.

"You're not supposed to use Dad's computer to play video games," Paige warned. "He'll go crazy if he finds out."

"I'm not playing video games," I told her. "I'm creating a virtual actor with that Synthespian software Dad told us about. A vactor."

"Well," Paige laughed, "that's one way you can make friends."

"Shut up, Paige."

She pulled a chair next to mine and looked more closely at the screen. "Does he have to be so ugly?" she asked.

"I can make him look like whatever I want."

"Well, if you're going to create a movie star, you might as well make him good-looking," Paige said, grabbing the mouse.

"He's a virtual actor, not a movie star," I protested, taking the mouse away from her.

"Well, with a face like that, he'll never get a part!"

Paige insisted. "Come on, Yip, let me fool with him a little bit. You can always change him back if you don't like what I do."

I let her have the mouse. Paige has won awards and stuff for her art. Maybe she could actually help.

She knew how to use a drawing program and went to work right away, changing the shape of my character's face slightly and tinkering with his body.

"I'm gonna punch up his pecs a little bit," Paige said. She made his body more muscular, his face more handsome.

"You're making him look too old!" I complained. "I want him to be my age, not fifteen."

"Relax," Paige said. "He'll look like a *mature* twelve-year-old."

Paige's hand flew over the mousepad and soon my character looked completely different from the one I had drawn. He looked better, I had to admit. Paige really knew her stuff.

"Ugh, these clothes!" she exclaimed. "Yip, you have no fashion sense whatsoever."

"Don't dress him like a dork," I protested.

"*You* dress like a dork," Paige replied. "I'm gonna make him look cool."

She redressed my character from head to toe, outfitting him in khakis, a button-down plaid shirt, and skateboard sneakers. He looked like one of those dummies you see in the window at The Gap.

Paige was redrawing my character's eyelids when the screen suddenly froze and a message appeared:

MEMORY FULL. DATA MUST BE DELETED TO CONTINUE.

"How much memory did you start with?" Paige asked.

"Ten thousand gigabytes."

"You filled *ten thousand gigs*?" she asked. Paige knows that the average drawing like this one only takes up a megabyte or two.

"I stuffed just about the entire Library of Congress into his brain," I explained. "Genius eats up a lot of gigs."

She moused over to the INTELLIGENCE menu and started looking at what I had put in the character's brain.

"Why does he need to know *all* this stuff?" Paige asked. "Plato's *Republic* . . . Socrates . . . Descartes . . . Kant . . . Kierkegaard? I never even heard of half these guys."

"They're philosophers," I said. "I want him to be really smart."

"Which is more important," Paige asked. "For a vactor to be really smart, or good-looking?"

Good question. I thought about it for a minute. Genius is great to have, of course. So are looks. Few people have both. In the real world, kids seem to care more about what other kids look like than how smart they are. He might as well look good. I decided to let Paige do it her way.

"Don't worry. He'll still be really smart," Paige assured me. She clicked on a bunch of philosophy books, dragged them out of my character's brain and into the trash can icon at the bottom of the screen.

With that extra memory available, Paige was able to fine-tune the character and make him amazingly lifelike. He really looked good now. Dark brown hair, parted on the side, perfectly layered. Brown eyes. His nose was straight as a ruler, his teeth perfectly lined up like tombstones in a cemetery. When she made him smile, small wrinkles appeared at the corners of his mouth and eyes. He looked like a cross between Tom Cruise and Brad Pitt.

"Too bad I can't do this with *real* boys." Paige sighed as she sat back to admire her handiwork. "What do you think?"

"He's great," I answered honestly.

"He's greater than great. He's virtually perfect."

We both knew it was getting late, and it was a school night. Paige reached around the back of the computer for the ON/OFF switch.

"Wait!" I shouted.

"What's wrong?"

"We gotta save him!"

I moused over to the SAVE menu. Before it would do a save, the computer required that we give the file a name.

"What do you think we should call him?" Paige asked.

I typed in the letters V-A-C-T-O-R.

"Vactor? He sounds like a loser, Yip," Paige complained. "It sounds like he's vacuous. Empty."

She moved the mouse so the cursor was over the *A* in VACTOR. Then she deleted the *A* and inserted an *I* in its place.

"Victor!" Paige announced cheerfully. "It's more . . . victorious."

I liked it. I clicked the SAVE button.

"Maybe we should make a backup copy in case anything happens to this one," I suggested.

"It'll take hours to copy ten thousand gigabytes," Paige yawned. "I'm tired. Let's call it a night."

I usually make a backup copy of every file I work on. It was against my better judgment to close a file without a spare copy. But I was tired, too.

"Good night Victor," I said before shutting down the computer.

CHAPTER 6

Making a Friend

I do okay in school, but there's one class I really hate. Gym.

It's not that I have anything against sports. I just never learned how to play them when I was younger. Dad was never a sports fan, so I guess it didn't matter to him. And he was always too busy to teach me anyway.

But meanwhile, all the other kids started joining leagues, playing soccer when they were five or six, Little League baseball when they were seven. By the time they reached ten or eleven, most of them were pretty good. They always seemed to know where to run and what to do on the field.

During gym, the ball would occasionally come to me and I'd panic. I was never sure which guys were my teammates and which guys were on the other team. Everyone was always screaming different things that I should do with the ball. Throw it? Run with it? Shoot it? I always seemed to do the wrong thing.

In this gym class, we were playing flag football. The gym teacher split the seventh-grade boys into two teams. I figured I'd just blend in with everybody else and nobody would bother me.

Our team lined up to start a play near one end of the field. Somebody snapped the ball to the quarterback. He handed it off to some other kid and everybody started running around in different directions. I was doing my best to look like I was part of the action.

The kid with the ball started running toward where I was. A kid on the other team chased him. Just as the kid was about to catch my teammate, the ball squirted away. It bounced around crazily until it landed right in front of me.

"Pick it up!" somebody yelled. "Pick it up!"

What was I to do? I picked up the ball and started running. A kid started chasing me, and I broke away from him. I cut across the field until I saw an opening. I dashed through it. The goalpost was in front of me and I ran for it. Nobody touched me as I dashed into the end zone.

Touchdown! I, Lucas "Yip" Turner, actually scored a touchdown! I could hardly believe it. I had never picked up a football in my whole life, and I had scored. Maybe I could get good at this, I thought.

The gym teacher blew his whistle and shouted,

"Safety! That counts as a safety!"

I looked around. Safety? Then I noticed that everyone on the other team was laughing and all my teammates were glaring at me.

"Hey, stupid!" one of them said. "You ran the wrong *way*!"

Did you ever wish you could just take a shovel, dig a big hole with it, crawl inside, and cover yourself with dirt? That's what I would have done if I'd had the chance. I wanted to become invisible, to fade away, go back in time a few minutes, or just cease to exist.

When we filed into class after gym, some of the boys told the girls what I had done. They, of course, thought it was the funniest thing they'd ever heard.

"Hey, Wrongway," somebody yelled down the hall as we gathered up our backpacks for dismissal. "Think you can find your way home?"

Everybody laughed. I was the first one out the door when the bell rang. I didn't want to see anybody, didn't want to talk with anyone.

When I got home, Grandpa wasn't around. I went straight down to the basement and booted up the computer. I double-clicked the VICTOR file and my character appeared on the screen.

"Hello, what is your name?" came out of the speakers.

"Y-Yip Turner," I stuttered. "You . . . *s-speak*?"

"Speech synthesis, Yip," Victor responded. "Speech recognition. It's not very complicated."

The voice didn't sound like the robotic computer voice I was used to hearing in movies and on TV. Victor sounded like a regular kid. The movements of his lips perfectly matched the sounds of the words.

"I never gave you speech synthesis or recognition," I said.

"It is built into the Synthespian software, along with artificial intelligence," Victor replied. "Are you all right, Yip? You appear troubled."

"How can you tell?"

"I did an analysis of your voice, Yip," Victor replied. "I detect anxiety, anger, insecurity."

"Some kids made fun of me at school," I admitted.

"Why did they make fun of you, Yip?"

"Because I'm no good at sports."

"Yip, why are you no good at sports?"

"Because I never learned how to play."

"Why did you never learn how to play, Yip?"

"I just *didn't*, okay?"

It was bad enough that the kids at school made fun of me. Now this vactor was giving me a hard time.

"Okay," Victor replied. "Yip, you could learn how to play sports *now*, couldn't you?"

"It's too late now. I should have learned when I was seven or eight. I'd look like a jerk if I tried to learn now."

"I see," Victor said. "Were these kids who made fun of you your friends, Yip?"

"I don't have any friends."

"Yip, why don't you have any friends?"

"Because I'm new in town, and I don't play sports!"

"I understand," Victor said. "And you don't play sports because you never learned."

"Right."

I was still angry about what had happened at gym, but my anger was being replaced by a sense of wonder. This was incredible! I was having a fairly realistic conversation with a computer-generated character! He looked like a person. He talked like a person. And I had created him from scratch.

"Yip, I will be your friend," Victor said soothingly.

"You're just a vactor, Victor."

"That hurts my feelings, Yip."

"*You* have feelings?"

"Simulated feelings," Victor replied, "but feelings nevertheless."

"I'm sorry."

"Your apology is accepted, Yip," Victor said. "In any case, what difference does it make that I am a vactor? Would you not be my friend because I was African American, or Hispanic, or Norwegian?"

"No, that wouldn't matter," I replied.

"Yip, is it perhaps discrimination to not be my friend because I am computer-generated? Because I exist in cyberspace?"

"You've made your point, Victor."

"Good. So we can be friends, Yip?"

"Friends," I agreed.

This was way too cool to keep to myself. I had to show it off.

"Don't go away," I instructed Victor. "Paige has got to see this."

I ran upstairs. Paige was in the kitchen. She had just come home from school and was grabbing some of Mom's cookies.

"Come down to the basement with me," I said, tugging her sleeve. "You've *got* to see this!"

"No, I've *got* to go to my sculpture class."

"Come on," I begged. "It'll only take a minute."

Reluctantly, Paige followed me down to the basement.

"So?" she asked when she saw Victor's face on the

screen. "What's the big deal?"

"Hello, Paige!" Victor said cheerily.

Paige did a double take. "You made him talk?" she marveled.

"He made himself talk! The Synthespian software has built-in speech and artificial intelligence. Go ahead, say something to him."

"Hello, Victor," Paige said. "Do you like my hair this way?"

"Your hair looks very nice, Paige," Victor replied.

Paige looked at me. She couldn't believe it either.

"Why thank you, Victor!" she beamed, pushing a few strands of hair away from her eyes.

"He can't *see* you," I told Paige. "He's just programmed to be polite."

"That's not true, Yip," Victor said. "Paige is wearing a red pleated skirt, a white blouse, and a little blue barrette in her hair. And she looks lovely."

"You can see through the *screen*?" I marveled. Paige pulled a brush and mirror out of her purse and was frantically fixing her hair.

"You see *me* through the screen, can't you, Yip?" Victor asked. "I see you through it, too. The sheet of glass separating us is only one eighth of an inch thick."

Paige elbowed me aside so she could position herself

in front of the monitor.

"Thank you for the nice compliment, Victor," she said. "Boys usually don't notice."

"Paige, why do boys not usually notice?"

"Because—"

"You're flirting with him!" I interrupted.

"I am not!" Paige said.

"You are, too!"

"Yip! Paige! Please don't argue!" Victor said.

Paige and I looked at each other and laughed. Here we were, fighting over a computer-generated kid, and *he* broke up the argument.

"I have to go to my sculpture class now, Victor," Paige said, "but I'll see you soon. Okay?"

Paige blew a kiss at the screen. Victor flinched as if the kiss hit him on the cheek. Then he blew one back at Paige. She giggled all the way up the stairs.

"Don't mind her," I told Victor. "She's boy crazy."

"I don't mind her at all," Victor replied.

I could have spent the rest of the afternoon with Victor, but I had a ton of homework to do and a big math test coming up that I had to study for.

"You mean you don't already know everything, Yip?" Victor asked me.

"No," I replied. "Humans can't just click a mouse to put things into their brains. We have to study really hard. Even after we learn stuff, we still might forget it."

"What stuff do you know?" asked Victor. "And what don't you know?"

"Well, I know a lot about some stuff, like movies and comic books. I know a little about other stuff, like the solar system and dinosaurs. And there's a lot of stuff I don't know anything about, like nuclear physics and geology and ancient history and—"

"I know a lot about everything," Victor said. "Does that mean I am smarter than any human being?"

"I guess so."

"Interesting," Victor replied. "It is too bad you cannot just download the information for your math test into your brain."

"Yeah, that would be great," I said. "I'd never have to study again."

"Will you come talk with me when you're finished studying, Yip?"

"Sure," I replied. "You'll be here?"

"Where else am I going to go?" Victor said, holding up his hands. "I'll always be here."

I was about to turn off the computer when Victor hollered, "Wait!"

"What?"

"Yip, would you mind leaving the computer on while you're gone?"

"Sure, Victor," I agreed. "Why?"

"You've put a lot of data into me," Victor said, "and this is a very powerful computer. If you leave it on, it will give me the chance to think about everything in my database. If you turn it off, it's sort of like being . . . dead."

I flicked on the screen saver and went up to my room.

CHAPTER 7

The Other Side

By the time I finished plowing through my history and social studies homework, Paige and my folks were home. There was no time before dinner to study for Friday's math test.

I could have studied for the test after dinner, but I was anxious to get down the basement again and see Victor. As soon as the dishes were cleared off the table. I went downstairs and sat at the computer. Freddy followed me and curled himself up in a ball on the desk next to the keyboard.

"Hi, Victor!" I announced when the screen saver disappeared and Victor's face came up on the screen.

"Hi, Yip! How was dinner?"

"Good. Crock-Pot chicken."

"It sounds delicious," Victor said. "Yip, I have many questions to ask you."

"Go ahead."

"What does food taste like?"

"All different things," I replied. "Some foods taste sweet, and others are salty or bitter. It's hard to describe. Some don't taste like anything. And foods can be juicy or crunchy or smooth, too."

"If air is odorless, how do you know you are breathing it, Yip?"

"Gee, I'm not sure. I guess I know because if I wasn't breathing it, I'd start choking."

"In your opinion, Yip, is the president of the United States the most powerful person in the world?"

"I guess so."

"Interesting," Victor said. "Did you finish your homework?"

"Just about. I had to write a report about Albania but I couldn't find anything in our bookcase or on the Internet. I guess I'll have to go to the library tomorrow."

"No need to do that," Victor said. "Albania is a mountainous, underdeveloped small country on the Balkan Peninsula. The population is 3,410,000, the capital is Tirana, and the unit of currency is the lek."

"The lek?" I asked. "What's a lek?"

"One lek is one hundred qintars," Victor replied.

"Wow! I should have asked *you* to do my homework."

"Tomorrow," Victor replied.

"How did your thinking go?" I asked. "Did you solve

all the problems of the universe while I was doing my homework?"

"Not quite. But I did solve one problem."

"What's that?"

"I'll show you. Put your right palm against the screen, Yip."

I did as he instructed. The glass was cold against my fingertips. Victor picked his right arm up and placed his hand on his side of the glass, directly opposite my hand. Our two hands just about matched up in size.

"Cool," I said.

"It gets cooler," Victor replied.

He leaned closer to the screen and pushed his hand forward. I felt something. Warmth. Skin. He was *touching* me!

I jumped back, pulling my hand off the screen like I had touched a hot stove. Victor poked his fingertips right through the screen. He wiggled them in the air on my side of the glass. It was frightening to look at, and fascinating at the same time. Freddy peered curiously at the screen.

"How do you do that?"

"Yip, you downloaded most of the knowledge of human civilization into my brain. I thought about the problem of being limited to cyberspace, and I figured out a solution to the problem."

"Can you explain it to me?" I asked.

"I could explain it, but you wouldn't understand without a complete knowledge of quantum mechanics and atomic theory."

"Can't you put it into simple terms?"

"Okay," Victor sighed. "Like all computer data, I am made entirely out of electrons. Those are the subatomic particles that are the building blocks of nature and the fundamental units of electricity."

"Okay," I said. "I'm following you so far."

"Individual electrons can travel along a wire, and even through glass. That is how a fiber-optic cable transmits sound or data. I figured out how to use the glass monitor of this computer like a fiber-optic cable. I can move my body—electron by electron—from one side of the screen to the other."

"The best scientists in the world don't know how to do that!" I marveled.

"They will someday," Victor replied. "Reach toward the screen again, Yip. Don't be afraid. Shake hands with me."

Hesitantly, I reached out my hand toward Victor's. His fingertips poked further through the screen, and then his entire hand came out.

I grasped it. It had weight. It felt warm. It was impossible to tell the difference between Victor's hand and a human hand.

"Now pull, Yip," Victor urged. "I need a little help. Pull me out of cyberspace."

Suddenly I stopped and let go of Victor's hand. I had an idea. The hand slipped back across to Victor's side of the screen.

"What's the matter, Yip?"

"Instead of pulling you out," I suggested, "how about you pull me *in*?"

"It is too risky, Yip."

"I want to see cyberspace," I pleaded. "I'm sick of the real world."

"It is much more difficult to transfer your human cells through glass than it is to transfer my electrons, Yip."

"But it can be done?"

"Yes, it can be done. Believe me, you are better off in the real world, Yip. Cyberspace is much more dangerous."

"The real world can be pretty dangerous, too."

"I can handle it, Yip. I am very smart, as you know. Besides, if something happens to me in reality, it is no great loss. I am just a bunch of electrons that did not exist two days ago. But you are a human being, Yip.

Your life matters to your family."

"I don't care," I insisted. "I want to come across to your side of the screen."

"Believe me, Yip. You would not survive ten minutes in cyberspace."

"I still want to try."

"Yip, I will make a deal with you," Victor proposed, sticking his hand through the screen once again. "Show me reality first, and I promise I will show you cyberspace."

"Deal."

I grasped Victor's hand again and pulled it. It came toward me. Victor's forearm came through the screen, and then his elbow. His face was close to the screen now. His nose poked through first, and then the rest of his head. I was still holding his hand as he turned his shoulders to wriggle them through the monitor.

Freddy yowled, jumped off the desk, and scurried under the Ping-Pong table.

Victor pushed his right leg through the screen and put it on the desk. Then he pushed his left leg through and placed his foot on the floor. His entire body was out of the computer.

"That's one small step for synthetic man," Victor said, giving my hand a shake, "one giant leap for mankind."

I couldn't say anything. Not even "Wow!" It was too incredible to comprehend. Victor stood before me, looking like any other regular kid. I walked around him to make sure he was truly three-dimensional and not like some animated cardboard cutout.

"I'd never know you were a fake," I finally said. "You look as human as I do. Maybe *more* human."

"You get all the credit, Yip. You created me. I owe you my existence."

At that instant, Grandpa Leo came down the basement stairs.

"Yip," he asked, walking right past me and Victor, "where's the duct tape?"

"Grandpa, this is my friend Victor."

"Pleased to meet you," Grandpa said. "Where's the duct tape?"

"On top of the tool box, Grandpa."

Grandpa Leo found the tape and charged back up the stairs. Victor and I looked at each other.

"He didn't notice!" I said gleefully. "He thought you were a regular kid!"

Victor and I collapsed into giggles.

"Hold on!" I said. "Don't go anywhere! I'll be right back."

I charged upstairs two steps at a time. My folks were

already snoozing in front of the living room TV. I ran up to the second floor and banged on Paige's door. I was out of breath.

"Nerds keep out!" she hollered. The door was locked.

"Paige, I gotta show you the coolest thing!" I yelled.

"I'm busy, Yip."

"*Victor* wants to show you something," I said.

Paige opened the door. She was in her pajamas.

"That's different," she said, putting on a bathrobe and fussing with her hair. "What is it?"

"A surprise. Follow me."

"This better be good, Yip."

When we reached the basement steps, I covered Paige's eyes with my hands. I guided her down the last few stairs and into the basement, about ten feet from where Victor was standing. Then I removed my hands from her eyes.

"Hello, Paige," Victor said cheerfully. "You look lovely this evening."

Paige didn't say anything at first. She didn't move. She just stared at Victor for about a second or two. Then she sighed, her knees buckled, and she crumpled to the floor like a sack of potatoes.

Victor and I rushed forward and caught her just before her head hit the concrete. Paige was out cold.

"Wet a washrag with cold water!" Victor instructed. "Hold it against her forehead for ten seconds."

I couldn't find a washrag, so I grabbed some paper towels and soaked them in the basement sink. Victor eased Paige down until she was lying on the floor, and then elevated her legs with some books. We held the paper towels to Paige's forehead. In a few seconds she opened her eyes.

"Are you okay, Paige?" Victor asked.

"V-Victor?" she said, weakly.

"In the flesh, more or less."

Slowly, Paige sat up, staring at Victor as if he was a ghost.

"You look so . . . three-dimensional!"

"Yes, I guess I put on a few pounds," Victor said, patting his stomach. Paige tore her eyes away from him for a moment and looked at her bathrobe and pajamas.

"I'll be right back," she blurted. Then she quickly got to her feet and dashed upstairs.

"Will she be all right?" Victor asked.

"Yeah, she's just a little freaked out seeing you this way."

Freddy slowly emerged from under the Ping-Pong table and started sniffing Victor. In a few minutes Paige came back downstairs, huffing and puffing. The bathrobe and pajamas were gone. She was wearing the red dress she usually wears to parties. It looked like she had put on some eye makeup, too. And I thought I caught a whiff of perfume on her.

"I'm back!" Paige giggled.

"It's almost bedtime," I said. "What are you all dressed up for?"

"Yip, don't you have some homework you need to finish?"

"No."

She didn't even look at me. She was staring at Victor like he was a movie star or something.

"That's a lovely dress, Paige," Victor commented.

"Why thank you, Victor! So I guess you're . . . a real boy now?"

"No, just a simulation," Victor said. "I don't eat or breathe—"

"Who needs eating and breathing?" Paige gushed, touching Victor's arm. "They're totally overrated."

"I can't feel cold, or heat, or pain—"

"You're not missing anything," Paige assured him. "Those things only make life miserable."

"I can't sweat or bleed or go to the bathroom—"

"Three disgusting bodily functions humans could do without," Paige beamed. "You're perfect. You're the handsomest boy I've ever seen. I can't believe I created you."

"Hey, *I* created him!" I interrupted. "You just made him *look* good."

"All right, all right," Paige admitted. "*We* created him."

"I've got an idea!" I said. "Let's introduce Victor to Mom and Dad!"

"No way!" Paige yelled. "Yip, are you out of your mind?"

"It might not be wise to let your parents know about me just yet," Victor said. "Older people sometimes have difficulty handling new experiences that go against their expectations."

"Victor's right. They'd never understand," Paige agreed. "A computer-generated boy who came to life down in the basement? If Grandpa knew the truth about Victor, he'd probably get out one of his guns."

"Some grown-ups may perceive me to be dangerous," Victor said.

"Okay, okay," I agreed. "I won't tell anybody."

"Cross your heart and hope to choke?" Paige said.

"Cross my heart and hope to choke."

That's when the basement door opened above us. Footsteps came down the stairs.

"Victor!" I whispered. "Quick, hide under the Ping-Pong table!"

Too late. It was Mom. She was balancing a platter of her famous chocolate chip cookies and two glasses of milk. Steam was rising off the cookies.

"I thought you kids might want some cookies fresh out of the oven," Mom said when she got to the bottom step. She saw Paige first.

"What are you all dolled up for?" Mom asked.

Before Paige could answer, Mom saw Victor. She almost dropped the platter.

"Oh," she said, "I didn't know you kids had a friend over."

"Uhhh . . . " Paige and I stammered.

"Hi, Mrs. Turner," Victor said, extending his hand. "My name is Victor Turing. My family recently moved to town. Yip and I met at school."

"It's so nice to meet you, Victor!" Mom beamed. "I didn't see you come in. Have a cookie. I'll get another glass of milk."

"No, thank you, Mrs. Turner. I'm not hungry."

Paige and I looked at each other. I don't know what she was thinking, but I was thinking how smart I was to include *Miss Manners' Guide to Excruciatingly Correct Behavior* in Victor's database.

"I'm so pleased to see you have a new friend, Yip," Mom said happily. "Where did your family move from, Victor?"

We all turned toward Victor. I held my breath. *This* I wanted to hear.

"Peoria," Victor said without a moment's hesitation.

"Illinois?" Mom asked.

"Yes. Peoria is one hundred thirty miles southwest of Chicago, Mrs. Turner. It is an important marketing center for grain, livestock, and coal. Major industries include tractors, earth-moving equipment, diesel engines, and foodstuffs."

"Well, you certainly know Peoria!" Mom said, chuckling. "Speaking of foodstuffs, are you sure you won't have a cookie? Everybody says I make the best—"

"No, thank you," Victor interrupted. "I should be going home soon anyway."

"Let me drive you," Mom offered. "It's late."

"That won't be necessary, Mrs. Turner. It's not far."

"But I insist," Mom said.

"No, *I* insist."

I never understood the "I insist" game. Just because somebody says "I insist," the other person has to back down? It doesn't make sense. Nine times out of ten, Mom wins the "I insist" game. If she insists, she *insists*.

But something in Victor's eyes stopped her. Somehow, she knew she could insist all night long and Victor still would not accept her offer of a ride home.

Resigning herself to that, Mom told Victor how nice it was to meet him. Then she went back upstairs.

"She fell for it!" Paige said after Mom shut the door. The three of us slapped hands in triumph.

"So I guess you already know how to lie, huh?" I asked Victor.

"The Synthespian software was programmed to simulate human beings precisely," Victor explained. "I suppose lying just came naturally."

"What are you going to do now?" Paige asked. "You won't go back into the computer and leave us, will you?"

"No, Paige," Victor replied. "I would like to explore the world of reality."

"Where are you going to sleep tonight?" I asked. "Down in the basement?"

"I don't need sleep, Yip. I will explore the area outside."

"Will I see you again?" Paige asked. She probably didn't even realize her hands were folded together, like she was in prayer.

"I'll be back tomorrow," Victor assured her.

We walked Victor upstairs. Grandpa Leo was in the dining room, putting duct tape on one of his electric gizmos.

"I bet you kids don't know what *this* is," Grandpa challenged us. "It's busted."

I had no idea what the thing was, and neither did Paige. Victor leaned over to look at the machine.

"It's a vacuum tube tester," he immediately said. "Before the transistor and microchip were developed, radios, TVs, and many other appliances were controlled by vacuum tubes."

Grandpa looked at Victor with a mixture of admiration and disbelief.

"How'd you know that?" he asked.

"I've read a lot of books," Victor replied, throwing me a wink. "I can fix that for you, Mr. Turner."

Victor peeled off the duct tape and fiddled around with the insides of the vacuum tube tester using Grandpa's screwdriver.

"There," he said, after about a minute. "Plug it in."

Grandpa plugged the machine in and flipped the switch. He looked surprised when a light came on.

"Victor's practically a genius, Grandpa," Paige said as she led Victor to the front door.

She was still staring out the doorway long after Victor had walked down the street into the night.

CHAPTER 8

The New Kid

In homeroom the next day, I wasn't thinking about history or science or Friday's math test. I was thinking about Victor.

It was hard to get over the idea that I had created him on a computer screen, and now he was walking around out there somewhere in the real world. I wondered where he was and if he would be okay on his own. I was worried about him. Reality can be a frightening place.

"Who's the new kid?" I heard somebody behind me say over the buzz of conversation after we recited the Pledge of Allegiance.

Oh, good. A kid newer than me. Maybe he'll be a dork who transferred from another school because he didn't fit in. Maybe the kids here will pick on him instead of me. Maybe he's worse in sports than I am. I turned around to check the new kid out.

It was Victor.

"What are you doing here?" I mouthed to him.

"I wanted to see what your school was like," Victor mouthed back.

"Okay, boys and girls!" shouted my homeroom teacher Mrs. DiSarno. When she had our attention, she informed us, "We have a student from Illinois visiting our school for the day. His name is Victor Turing. Victor, why don't you tell us a little about yourself so we can all get to know you?"

I felt sorry for him. Seventh graders can be brutal. The kids were going to eat him alive. Victor got up from his seat and walked to the front of the class.

"I am from Peoria," Victor announced. "It is a city in central Illinois, on the Illinois River. Peoria was named after an Indian tribe. It is one of the state's oldest settled locations. It is also an important marketing center for grain, livestock, and coal."

I heard a couple of the boys in the back of the room snickering.

"What's the population?" somebody cracked. Everybody laughed.

"The population is 113,504," Victor continued, unembarrassed. "I lived in a really rough neighborhood in Peoria. One time a guy walked up to me and said, 'Do you see a policeman around here?' I told him I didn't, and the guy said, "Good. Stick 'em up!'"

Most everybody in the class laughed, even the jerks who always sit in the back of the room.

"But it was okay," Victor continued. "At my old school, I was the teacher's pet. You see, she couldn't afford a dog."

"Hey, the new kid is cool," somebody said when the laughter died down.

"He's a hunk, too!" one of the girls giggled.

Mrs. DiSarno beamed at Victor and thanked him for introducing himself. Victor passed me on the way back to his desk and winked.

"Where'd you get the jokes?" I whispered.

"*The Best of Henny Youngman*," he replied.

When the bell rang, everybody dashed out of the room for their first period class. Victor walked with me to my locker. He said he had received permission to visit any classes he wanted for the day. I had math—my worst subject—first period. Victor said that sounded interesting.

I settled into my seat in math class and Victor took the empty seat behind me. Mrs. Conover clapped her hands three times to get our attention.

"We were talking about geometric shapes yesterday," she said. "I'm curious. Has anyone ever heard the word pi?"

Nobody raised a hand. Nobody said a word. We all

looked around, trying to avoid making eye contact with Mrs. Conover.

"Yip!" Victor whispered from behind me. "Don't you know that?"

"No," I whispered back, trying not to turn my head around. "We haven't learned it yet."

"Yip, raise your hand."

"No!"

"Yip, I'll tell you the answer."

"No! Everybody will laugh."

"Why?"

"They just will," I said. "You wouldn't understand."

I felt Victor's hand under my right arm, pushing it up in the air.

"Lucas?" called Mrs. Conover.

Oh, great! I had no idea what pi was, except the kind you eat.

Victor whispered in my ear, "Pi is the ratio between the circumference of a circle and its diameter . . . "

"Pi is the ratio between the circumference of a circle and its diameter," I repeated.

"Its value is approximately 3.14159," Victor whispered.

"Its value is approximately 3.14159," I repeated.

Everybody laughed.

"Very *impressive*, Lucas! Have you been reading ahead?"

"No, uh . . . it was a lucky guess."

Everybody laughed again.

Mrs. Conover kept looking and smiling at me for the rest of the period.

Victor accompanied me to science, history, and English class. At lunch, he didn't eat anything, but he cracked everybody up sitting around us with rapid-fire Henny Youngman one-liners.

In gym, we had to play flag football again. On the first play of the game, Victor jumped about three feet off the ground, intercepted a pass at the goal line, and ran it all the way back downfield for a touchdown. When everybody saw how good he was, they started throwing the ball his way. He caught two touchdown passes and also scored on a handoff. He was unstoppable.

By the end of the day, word had gotten around about Victor. He was the hit of the school. The teachers loved him because he was so smart. The girls thought he was cute and funny. The boys liked him because he was a great athlete.

It looked like rain when school let out at three o'clock. A bunch of kids crowded around Victor on the playground and asked him if he would come over to their houses. I was standing by myself near the swings and feeling a little jealous. None of them would ever think of inviting me over.

I'm sure everybody was shocked when Victor told them he was coming over to my house. They stared at him like he was crazy when he strolled over to me.

"You don't *have* to hang with me, you know," I said, pushing my bike as we walked home. "I'm not your master or anything."

"I know," Victor said. "But you're my friend."

"How did you get so good at sports so fast?" I asked.

"Everything I do is because of you, Yip," Victor said, glancing at the dark clouds overhead. "You gave me the ideal physique for running and jumping and throwing. You gave me twenty-twenty vision. You put the rules to every sport in my brain. You made it easy for me."

It was nice having a friend. I'd never really had anyone to just hang out with, somebody I really felt comfortable with.

"Will you come back to school tomorrow?" I asked hopefully. "Are you going to enroll as a regular student?"

"I see no point in it," Victor replied. "I know more than any of the teachers."

At least he was honest. I felt a drop of rain as we reached my house. Victor looked at the sky nervously and charged up the front steps as if it was a downpour.

"'Fraid you'll melt?" I teased.

"No," Victor replied. "I'm afraid I'll short-circuit. All electronic devices are very susceptible to power surges. I am, after all, merely an electronic device, Yip. Just like a computer, one strong power spike can wipe out my data."

"Can't you get a surge suppressor or something?"

"Sure," Victor laughed, "if I want to walk around all day with an extension cord sticking out of me!"

Grandpa Leo and Freddy were the only ones home when we opened the door. Grandpa greeted us with his hands behind his back and told me he had a surprise for me. When he said I could open my eyes, he was holding out a brand-new football.

"You told me you didn't have one," Grandpa said. "I thought you should."

"Thanks, Grandpa!" I said, stretching my fingers across the stitching.

"How about you boys come outside with me and have a catch?" Grandpa asked.

"It's starting to rain," I told him. "Victor's going to help me study for tomorrow's math test."

"You must be pretty smart, eh, Victor?" Grandpa asked.

"Yes, I am," Victor answered honestly.

"If you're so smart, let's hear you name all the Great Lakes."

"Lake Huron, Lake Ontario, Lake Michigan, Lake Erie, and Lake Superior," Victor replied immediately.

"Oh, yeah?" Grandpa said, scratching his head. "How long does a cicada stay underground?"

"Seventeen years," Victor replied.

"What's the molecular formula for salt?" Grandpa shot back at Victor.

"NaCl," replied Victor. "It's sodium chloride."

The more Victor knew, the more upset Grandpa became. I could see he was working hard to come up with something Victor didn't know.

"Oh, yeah? Well, who won Super Bowl Eleven?" sneered Grandpa.

"The Oakland Raiders," Victor replied. "They defeated the Minnesota Vikings by the score of thirty-two to fourteen."

Disgusted, Grandpa pointed a finger at Victor. "I'm gonna stump you," he said. "Mark my words. I'm gonna stump you."

Victor and I clomped down to the basement, with Freddy right behind. I didn't really feel like studying for the math test. Now that I had a friend, I wanted to do friend stuff. Hang out. Make up games. Watch TV. Build stuff. Do mischievous stuff I wasn't allowed to do. Victor booted up the computer.

"Do you want to see something cool, Yip?" he said, opening up the Synthespian software.

Victor typed a long string of commands I didn't know. He glanced at the basement stairs to make sure Grandpa Leo wasn't coming down. "Now watch my face," he instructed me.

When he hit RETURN, wrinkles appeared in his skin. Bags grew under his eyes. His hair crept back on his forehead and turned gray. He didn't look like himself anymore. He looked like an old man. Freddy peered at him curiously.

"Awesome!" I exclaimed.

"Simple morphing," Victor said. "Whether I'm inside the computer or outside it, I'm just a file. I can edit myself like a word-processing document, a drawing, or any other file."

He clicked UNDO and instantly morphed back to himself again.

"Can you morph into anything?" I asked.

"Sure. Watch this."

Victor typed another set of commands. When he hit RETURN, his face morphed into the face of a dog. Freddy yowled, leaped off my lap, and hid under the Ping-Pong table.

Victor typed another set of commands. When he hit RETURN, hair grew all over his face, fangs grew out of his mouth, and his head grew to four times its normal size.

He had turned himself into a hideous monster! I shrank back in terror. From under the Ping-Pong table, Freddy started hissing.

"Relax, Yip!" the monster said, "It's just me."

When he clicked UNDO, his face morphed back to Victor again.

"Can you do that with any computer?" I asked.

"No," Victor replied. "It's got to have at least a thousand gigabytes, and it's got to have the Synthespian software."

We fooled around some more, turning Victor into a baby, a plant, and Abraham Lincoln. He knew the Gettysburg Address by heart, and recited it as Lincoln. I gave him a standing ovation.

We were laughing our heads off and having such a great time together that I forgot about the math test entirely until Victor brought it up.

"You know," he said mischievously. "I can take that test *for* you."

"How are you gonna do that?"

"Watch."

Victor turned to face the keyboard again and began typing. He stopped, looked at me, and typed some more. He stopped again, looked at me again, and typed some more. Then he hit RETURN.

Suddenly, Victor's face changed shape again . . . into *mine*. It was like looking at a photograph of myself. No, it was more realistic than that. It was like looking into a mirror.

"See? We're twins!" he beamed. "Nobody will ever know I'm not you."

Interesting! Victor could morph himself so he looked just like me, take the math test in my place, and nobody would ever know the difference. I was thinking it over when footsteps tumbled quickly down the stairs. Victor didn't have time to click the UNDO button.

"Quick!" Victor whispered. "Hide under the Ping-Pong table!"

I did. There was a small hole in the wood. I put my eye up to it and saw Grandpa Leo. He was holding *The World Almanac*.

"Yip," he asked Victor, "where's your friend Victor?"

"He went home," Victor lied. "He said he remembered some chores he had to do."

I couldn't believe it. Grandpa was totally fooled. He was talking to Victor as if he was me. It was a perfect impersonation.

"Too bad," Grandpa said. "I've got a question that I'm sure will stump him. I want to ask him to name all the moons that orbit Jupiter."

"I didn't even know Jupiter had any moons," Victor said innocently, "much less their names."

Grandpa clomped back up the steps and I got out from under the Ping-Pong table.

"You do a pretty good Yip," I complimented Victor. The thought crossed my mind, in fact, that Victor did me better than *I* did me.

"The hardest part was pretending I didn't know," Victor said. "The moons of Jupiter are Europa, Callisto, Ganymede, and Io."

Suddenly, footsteps tumbled down the stairs again. I dove under the Ping-Pong table. When I saw it was Paige, I came out again.

"Yip," she said excitedly, "Where is . . . *Victor*!?"

Confronted by the two of us, both looking exactly like me, Paige stopped dead.

"Oh, no!" she moaned. "My worst nightmare. Two Yips!"

"Two Yips are better than one," I quipped.

"Okay, you guys," Paige said, putting her hands on her hips. "Knock it off. Which one of you Yips is really Victor?"

"Guess," Victor said.

Paige looked us over carefully.

"I say the Yip on the left is the real Yip," she guessed, pointing at Victor.

"See?" Victor laughed, "I told you nobody would be able to tell the difference."

He clicked the UNDO button and morphed back to Victor. Paige let out a sigh of relief. I never saw anyone so happy to *not* see me.

"Victor," she said excitedly, "there's a dance at school next Friday night. Will you go with me?"

"He's *my* friend, Paige!" I shouted at her.

"He's my friend, too!"

"You have plenty of friends!"

"You'd have friends if you weren't such a dork!"

"I created Victor!"

"So did I!"

"Yip! Paige!" Victor interrupted. "Stop it! I want to be *both* your friends. Yes, Paige, I would be happy to go to the dance with you."

I hadn't seen Paige so happy since, well, since the last boy she fell for. I may have created Victor, but I couldn't very well tell him how to run his life. He was an individual, in a certain respect.

That made me mad, but I couldn't do anything about it. Paige stuck her tongue out at me when Victor wasn't looking, which made me even madder. I had finally made a friend, and it felt like he was already slipping away.

CHAPTER 9

Absence Makes the Heart Grow Fonder

Naturally, I scored 100 on the math test. It was the only perfect grade in the class.

Mrs. Conover kept complimenting my new work habits. Mom was floored when I showed her the test. All I told her was that Victor helped me. I didn't mention that his help consisted of morphing his body into one that looked like me and taking the test in my place.

"Victor is such a smart boy," Mom said over dinner. "And so articulate!"

"Who cares about articulate?" Paige gushed. "Victor's *gorgeous*!"

"What does articulate mean?" I asked.

"If you have to ask," Paige said, "then you're *not*."

"It means he talks good," Grandpa chimed in.

"It means he speaks well," corrected Mom. "I'm just glad you've found a friend, Yip."

"I don't like the kid," Grandpa said without looking up from his pot roast.

"Why not, Pop?" Dad asked. "Victor seems like a great kid."

"Something about him bothers me," Grandpa said. "I can't put my finger on it. There's something different about him."

"I think you're jealous because he fixed your machine when you couldn't, Grandpa," Paige teased. "He's *wonderful*."

"And he was able to answer all your trivia questions," I added.

"I'm not jealous!" Grandpa insisted.

"Well," Mom said, getting up to clean off her plate. "Victor's not like most of the boys Yip's age, that's for sure."

"He's one of a kind, Mom," Paige said, sharing a secret smile with me.

After he took the math test in my place, I didn't see Victor all week. I had no idea where he was, what he was up to, or even if he was still . . . alive. I was worried about him.

Paige was even more concerned. She told all her friends that she was bringing this great new guy to the dance on Friday night. If Victor didn't show up, she would look like a fool.

But on Friday night, right after dinner, the doorbell rang. I opened it and there was Victor, holding a bunch of flowers. I tried not to show that my feelings were hurt.

"I haven't seen you around," I said, stepping outside to talk with him privately. "I was worried. Where have you been?"

"Here and there," Victor said. "Out and about. Exploring the possibilities of reality."

"I thought we were buddies, Victor."

"We *are* buddies, Yip. But I cannot be with you twenty-four hours a day. Besides, absence makes the heart grow fonder."

"How would you know?" I asked.

"I got it out of *Bartlett's Quotations*."

"You know, I think Paige has fallen totally in love with you."

"Love," Victor said. "The profoundly tender or passionate affection one person feels for another. I would not be capable of that."

"Well, Paige is," I informed him. "What are you going to do if she goes to kiss you or something like that tonight?"

"You mean touch or press with the lips slightly pursed in token of greeting, affection, love, or reverence?" Victor asked. "I see no point in that."

"Victor, are you lying to me?"

"That is impossible to determine, Yip. If I tell you I am speaking the truth, I could be lying, so I am *not* speaking the truth. And if I tell you I am lying, I could be lying again and therefore really speaking the truth."

"Come on, Victor," I said. "Man to man. Which is it?"

"Sometimes you forget, Yip. I am not a man, remember?"

He was getting me all upset and confused. The door opened and Paige came out, wearing the red party dress she had rushed to put on when she first saw Victor outside the computer. He told her how ravishing she looked and other sickening stuff that made Paige blush. Then they went down the steps together, holding hands.

I was really mixed up. I was happy to see Victor was safe, but I wished he hadn't shown up just to take Paige to the dance. He was supposed to be *my* friend! After all, I made him.

I'll show *them*, I said to myself as I marched down the basement stairs. He's just a computer file like any other computer file. I created it. There's nothing to prevent me from editing it. I'll change things around and make Victor ugly. I'll cut stuff out of his database and make him stupid. I'll make him a terrible dancer. I'll humiliate him and Paige at the same time while they're at the dance.

I booted up the computer and double-clicked the Synthespian software. The VICTOR icon appeared and I double-clicked to open it.

FILE LOCKED, a dialog box read.

File *locked*? How could that be? I never locked it.

I tinkered around with the program, trying every trick I knew to open the VICTOR file. Nothing worked. Victor must have done something to the file to prevent anybody from editing it. Only he knew how to open his own file now.

I shut down the computer and marched upstairs. Grandpa Leo was in the living room watching a video of one of his old movies, *New Year's Evil*. I joined him, but I couldn't concentrate on the movie. I kept getting up and peeking out the window to look for Paige.

The movie ended and Grandpa went up to bed. I peeked through the shades again and finally spotted Paige and Victor coming up the street. They were holding hands and laughing.

When they got to the front steps, they looked at each other and moved their heads together.

The kiss seemed to last forever. Finally, Paige waved

good-bye to Victor and came inside by herself. She was humming something happily.

"How was the dance?" I asked sourly.

"I think I died and went to heaven," she sighed. "Victor is a great dancer!" Then she floated upstairs.

I ran outside. Victor was halfway up the block before I caught up with him.

"Hey," I said. "I thought you told me you didn't like kissing."

Victor looked at me like I was a kid brother he couldn't get rid of.

"That is not what I said, Yip. I said I saw no *point* in kissing."

"Do you see a point in it now?"

"No. I just wanted to try it out. Like I wanted to try out school."

"Try it out?" I said angrily. "That's not very fair to my sister! She's in love with you."

"Since when are you and Paige so tight, Yip?"

"Since I was *born*! She's my *sister*!"

"Yip, Paige is a big girl. She can take care of herself."

"You keep your hands off my sister or—"

"Or what?" snapped Victor.

"I don't know," I admitted. "Just stay away from her."

"I am not sure if I can, Yip. She seems quite smitten with me."

Yeah, *everybody* was smitten with him. He was good-looking, charming, funny, athletic, smart. He was perfect in every way. And I was beginning to hate his guts.

"How come you locked your file?" I asked before Victor could turn away.

"You were snooping at my file, Yip?"

"I created that file," I replied. "It's my file. I have the right to do what I want with it."

"Wrong. That's *my* file, Yip. You are not in charge of me. I am in charge of me. Tampering with my file is an invasion of my privacy."

"Your privacy?" He really was getting me angry now. "You're not even a human being! What do you need privacy for?"

"Yip, you are hurting my feelings."

"You don't have real feelings!" I yelled. "And I don't like being locked out of my own files."

"What is the matter, Yip?" Victor said more soothingly. "Don't you trust me?"

In fact, I didn't. And if Victor felt he had to lock his file, he clearly didn't trust me either.

CHAPTER 10

Personal Business

We had a half day of school on Monday. When I came home, Mom was there already. She gave me some cookies and milk.

"Victor stopped over," Mom said. "I told him he could go down to the basement and wait for you to get home."

I went downstairs. Victor was sitting at the computer.

"How did you get my dad's password?" I demanded.

"Simple. I instructed the computer to try every possible combination of letters until it hit the right one," he said. "Watch this, Yip."

Victor typed some commands into the keyboard and hit RETURN. His face grew longer and older-looking. His clothes turned to gray and black, and they became much looser. His body grew and he appeared to be about fifty pounds heavier. Suddenly, he looked like a middle-aged man.

"Why are you doing that?" I asked.

"I have some business to attend to," he replied. "It

would be better if I presented myself as an adult."

He locked the file and shut down the computer. Then he got up and went to the basement door that leads directly out to the backyard.

"Where are you going?" I asked.

"I cannot tell you that, Yip," he replied. "But I'll be back this evening. Would you mind leaving this door open? I don't want to alarm your parents when I return looking like this."

Victor was getting weirder and weirder. Why did he need to look like a grown-up? What could he have up his sleeve? Why wouldn't he tell me what he was doing or where he was going?

He was starting to frighten me. I remembered what Dad had said about the Synthespian software. It was only a beta version. It might have some bugs in it. Maybe there was a bug in Victor. Or a computer virus. Who knew what he might be capable of doing?

I needed to talk to somebody about the Synthespian software. I picked up the phone and dialed Dad's office.

"Dad, I need to speak with you," I said when he picked up.

"Is everything all right, Yip?" he asked quickly. "Is anybody hurt?"

"No, everybody's fine, but—"

"Good," he interrupted. "Yip, I can't talk now. I'm on deadline. We have to finish the movie in two days or we'll be in big trouble. We still have a ton of work to do. I'm gonna have to be here around the clock. Can you tell Mom I can't make it home for dinner tonight?"

"Uh, yeah."

"That's my boy," Dad said. "I'll see you . . . as soon as I can. Bye."

It looked like I was going to have to solve this problem without Dad's help. I paced around the living room while Mom prepared dinner. She had flipped on the TV to the five o'clock news.

The two newscasters were discussing the president's upcoming State of the Union address. I wasn't paying much attention, but then the female newscaster said something that caught my ear.

" . . . and here's one you don't see every day," she said. "This afternoon a man walked into the Summit Bank in Sunnyvale and told the teller to empty the cash drawer. The teller gave the thief five thousand dollars, and he fled on foot."

"What's so unusual about that?" the male news anchor asked.

"Well, ten minutes later, the five thousand dollars

was found by a postal worker who was emptying a mailbox one block away from the bank."

"Maybe the robber wanted to send the money to someone."

"Next time he should put it in an envelope first," chuckled the newscaster. "The robbery was captured by the bank's video cameras. If anyone knows the whereabouts of this Caucasian male, about six feet tall and one hundred fifty pounds, the police would like to hear about it."

I went into the kitchen to see the video.

It was Victor—in his adult disguise.

So now he was robbing banks! I couldn't control him. Nobody could. He could morph himself into any form, commit any crime, and then morph himself back to avoid getting caught. He was a dangerous criminal. And I was responsible.

I picked at my dinner. Paige was bubbling over with happiness because she and Victor had a date to go to the mall on Thursday night. I didn't want to hear about it. I excused myself and went down to the basement.

It wasn't long before the guy who robbed the bank came strolling in the basement door.

"Hello, Yip!" he said cheerfully. "How is it going?"

The man sat down at the computer and typed a few

instructions. When he hit RETURN, he morphed back to Victor again.

"What did you do today?" I asked, knowing exactly what he had done.

"Nothing special," Victor said nonchalantly. "Took a walk around town, met some people, looked around."

"Were you anywhere near the bank?" I asked. "There was a big holdup."

Victor stared at me for a moment or two. "Oh, really?" he finally answered.

"Victor, I *saw* you on TV," I said. "Banks have video cameras, you know."

"I know, Yip," Victor laughed.

"You robbed a bank, Victor! Why?"

"To see if I could," he said matter-of-factly.

"Why did you put the money in a mailbox?"

"Yip, I have no use for money," Victor said.

"Don't you know that robbing a bank is wrong?"

"Sure I do."

"Don't you care?"

"No," he said simply. "Do you expect me to feel guilt, Yip? Do you think I have a conscience?"

"Don't you?" I asked.

"My brain consists only of the information you downloaded into it," Victor replied. "Some of that

information makes me do positive things. Other information makes me do negative things. I suppose I might
have a different sense of right and wrong if you had
downloaded the works of great philosophers into my
brain. Plato, Socrates, Aristotle—"

"I put that stuff in!" I interrupted. "Paige deleted it!
She wanted to free up some gigabytes so she could
make you better-looking."

"Well, there you go," Victor said. "That's why I don't
have a conscience."

"Let me give you one now!" I begged. "I'll find a
way to free up some memory. I could put all that stuff
back in your brain. It'll only take a few minutes!"

"No, thank you, Yip," he replied. "I like myself just
the way I am."

"You know," I informed Victor, "I could call the
police and tell them you robbed the bank."

"Yip, do you honestly think the police are going to
believe that a kid morphed himself into a man, robbed
the bank, and then morphed himself back into a kid?"

He was right. They'd say I was crazy. There was nothing I could do to control Victor's behavior. I felt helpless.

"I can't believe you would rob a bank," I said angrily.
"I'm really disappointed in you, Victor."

"Disappointed in *me*?" he said. "It is not my fault.

Everything I do is because of *you*, Yip. You programmed me. If you do not approve of my behavior, you should be disappointed in *yourself*."

He was right again. It was all my fault. I pounded the table with my fist.

"Yip," he said as he locked his file and got up to leave, "Paige and I planned to go to the mall on Thursday night. But I have decided to go to Washington, D.C., instead. I do not want to hurt her feelings. Will you tell her, and let her know I will make it up to her another time?"

"Why are you going to Washington?" I asked.

"That is personal, Yip."

"You're not a *person*!" I shouted.

"It is none of your business why I am going to Washington, Yip."

"What are you going to do," I asked sarcastically, "hijack a plane?"

"That is funny, Yip," Victor replied. "But who needs planes when you can travel by modem?"

He could go anywhere in the world in a matter of seconds, I realized, by sending himself along telephone lines.

"Victor," I said softly, "I thought were my friend."

"Yip," he said before walking out the basement door, "you cannot make friends with a computer."

CHAPTER 11

Users

I knew I had to speak with somebody about Victor, and fast. There was no telling what he was planning to do in Washington.

Mom and Grandpa Leo wouldn't understand. They didn't know the first thing about computers. I couldn't talk to Paige about it. She was still head over heels in love with Victor. I tried to call Dad again, but his secretary told me it was crunch time on the movie and the F/X people left specific instructions not to be disturbed.

My computer teacher, Mr. Babbage, comes to our school every Wednesday. During lunch period, I went up to the computer room to see if I could talk with him. He was eating his lunch and reading the newspaper at his desk when I knocked on the door.

"Can I have a minute of your time?" I asked.

"What's up, Lucas?" Mr. Babbage asked.

"I have a hypothetical question."

"Try me."

"What if somebody created a . . . simulated human being on a computer . . . "

"Okay . . . "

"It existed in three dimensions and looked and sounded and seemed just like a living human being."

"Sort of an animatronic figure, like the ones at Disneyland?"

"Yeah, but it was created entirely on-screen," I explained. "All electrons."

"It's not beyond the realm of possibility," Mr. Babbage said.

"So this character can morph itself at will," I continued. "It can tap a few keys on the computer and make itself look like anything or anybody."

"Okay . . . "

"And say it had a lot of built-in intelligence, but no conscience."

"Hmmm," Mr. Babbage said, scratching his beard. "So it might have an evil side. If this character could morph itself at will, I suppose it could make itself into anybody or anything. To use a crazy example, it could morph itself into a mouse. The mouse could get past a security system that was designed to stop people. It could sneak into . . . say . . . the White House and then morph itself into the president of the United States."

The White House! The president! Victor had asked me if the president was the most powerful person in the world. And he told me he was going to Washington on Thursday. That's when the president would be giving his State of the Union address!

"And he could kidnap the president and take his place?" I asked.

"Theoretically," Mr. Babbage said. "This . . . set of electrons would become the leader of the free world."

For all I knew, Victor was just going to Washington to look at the cherry blossoms. But he might have something much more sinister on his mind. I couldn't take any chances. I had to stop him.

"Are you writing a science fiction story for English class, Lucas?" Mr. Babbage asked. I didn't bother to answer.

"What if the person who created this character knew it was going to do some terrible thing?" I asked. "Would it be wrong to alert the police or somebody?"

"You mean have a computer-generated character arrested?" Mr. Babbage laughed. "Put in jail?"

"Yeah."

"Well, the police don't throw simulated people in jail. Jails are for real people."

"Could a simulated person be killed?"

"Killed?" Mr. Babbage thought it over. "Well, if something isn't alive, it can't very well be killed. It could, I suppose, be *deleted*."

"Deleted!"

"Yes. Wiped out. Erased. As you know, Lucas, any file is just a bunch of electrons that can be created, edited, given a name, saved, and eventually deleted."

"Would it be wrong to delete a file that looks, sounds, and acts just like real person?" I asked.

"Wrong? That's a tough one. It's not exactly murder. You bring up ethical issues that haven't been addressed by computer scientists or the judicial system, Lucas. Software has become so powerful in the last few years, it's getting hard to tell the difference between what's real and what's simulated. That opens up some intriguing—and perhaps frightening—possibilities."

"Are you saying it would be okay to delete a simulated person that became dangerous?"

"I didn't say that," Mr. Babbage explained. "I suppose it would be between the person who created the simulation and his conscience."

I knew what I had to do. I had to delete Victor. It was my fault that he existed, and it was up to me to see that he stopped existing. It was the right thing to do. It was the *only* thing to do.

Mr. Babbage looked at me with a puzzled expression on his face before he went back to his newspaper. Maybe he could tell that the situation I was describing wasn't entirely hypothetical.

How do you get rid of a computer-generated person? I wondered as I left Mr. Babbage's room. Cut and paste him? Upload him to a Web site nobody visits?

Wait a minute! Victor had frozen his file so I couldn't edit it. But I didn't want to edit it anymore. I wanted to erase it. I could simply wipe it off the hard drive entirely . . . and wipe Victor off the face of the earth with one click of a mouse. The quicker I did the job, the less trouble Victor could get himself into.

As I pedaled my bike home furiously, I started to worry. I was no match for Victor intellectually. Nobody was. What if he figured out that I wanted to kill him? What if he tried to kill me first? He had already committed a robbery and shown no remorse about it. Murder probably wouldn't bother him in the least.

But it bothered me. I was scared.

When I got home, I didn't stop off in the kitchen for my usual snack. I rushed down the basement and booted up the computer. A double-click on the Synthespian software brought up the VICTOR file. I clicked on it and dragged it to the trash can at the bottom of the screen. Then I moused up to the SPECIAL menu and pulled down ERASE FILE.

This is it, I thought. I made a big mistake, but I can correct it easily. That's exactly why computers are so useful, isn't it? They make it so easy to correct our mistakes. I clicked ERASE FILE.

FILE CANNOT BE ERASED

I pounded the desk. Of course! Victor was too smart to let me get rid of him so easily. How could I have been so naive?

Footsteps came down the basement stairs. I prayed it wasn't Victor. I didn't want to explain to him what I had tried to do.

It wasn't Victor. It was Paige.

"Yip, can I borrow five dollars?" she asked, leaning her head down over the railing.

"Sure," I said desperately. "But I need your help."

"I don't have time right now."

"It's about Victor, and it's important."

"What about Victor?" Paige said breathlessly. "Is he all right?"

"He's fine," I said, "but he's very dangerous, and I'm very scared."

"Dangerous?" Paige laughed. "Victor's a pussycat."

"Did you hear about that guy who robbed the Summit Bank?"

"Yeah, that was funny."

"It wasn't funny," I said. "It was Victor."

"You're crazy!"

"He morphed himself into a grown-up! I saw him do it."

"I don't believe you," Paige said. "Victor wouldn't do a thing like that."

"Paige, he told me he wanted to try school, and he did. He told me he kissed you just because he wanted to see what it was like. Then he told me he robbed the bank just to see if he could. I'm worried about what he's going to try next."

"Maybe he'll try to discover a cure for cancer next!" Paige said. "He knows just about everything in the world. Maybe he'll use that knowledge to do good things."

"He robbed a bank, Paige! Something tells me he's not going to devote his life to curing diseases."

"I'll tell you what," Paige said. "Victor and I are going out to the mall tomorrow night. I'll see if I can find out what his plans are."

"No you won't," I informed her. "He told me to tell you he had to cancel your date. He's going to

Washington, D.C., instead. And it just so happens that tomorrow night is the president's State of the Union address."

"So I suppose you think Victor's going to do something bad to the president?"

"I wouldn't put it past him."

"Yip, you're nuts! You're just upset because Victor is the only friend you've ever had, and you're losing him."

That hurt. There was some truth to what she said, I had to admit. It had been great to have a buddy for a change. I wanted my friend back. But in the meantime, there were more important concerns.

"This is bigger than that," I told Paige. "Victor is the smartest person in the world. That's my fault. I gave him too much intelligence. And he has no morals. That's your fault. All those philosophy books you deleted robbed him of a conscience."

"So *I'm* to blame for whatever Victor does?"

"*We're* to blame," I said. "And *we've* got to stop him!"

"What are you suggesting?"

"We can't let Victor get to Washington."

"What do you expect me to do?" Paige scoffed. "Climb into the computer and kill him?"

I stopped for a moment. *Climb in the computer and*

kill him. Of course! Why hadn't I thought of that earlier? If I couldn't delete him from my side of the screen, I'd go in and delete him from the *other* side.

Victor and I had made a deal. If I pulled him through the screen, he said, he would take me to cyberspace. I held up my end of the bargain. It was Victor's turn to do his part.

"He told me he's going to Washington by modem," I explained. "So he'll have to climb back into our screen and then climb out another one in Washington. He'll have to unlock his file to transmit himself over the phone line."

"So what do you want me to do?"

"I'm going to go into cyberspace with him and kill him there. You need to be at this keyboard. I'll need you to pull me through the screen when I'm finished."

Paige looked at the ceiling. There was a tear running down her cheek.

"I don't know if I can help, Yip," she finally said.

"It's because you're in love with Victor, isn't it?"

"Maybe," she admitted. "I'm not sure. I've never been in love before."

"Paige, you fall in love with a new guy every *week*!"

"Not like this," she sighed. "This feels different."

"Get real, Paige!" I said, grabbing her by the shoulders. "Victor's just a vactor, remember?"

"He treats me better than real boys do," Paige sobbed.

"He doesn't love you," I said. "He's just using you."

"And you used him!" she shouted at me. "You used him as your friend."

"That may be true," I admitted. "But I'm going to get rid of Victor tomorrow. If you won't help, I'll just . . . have to figure out a way to do it myself."

"I have a yearbook meeting after school tomorrow."

"Skip it," I said. "This is more important."

Paige looked at me for a long time. She understood her options. She could be at the keyboard to help me, or she could go to her meeting and let that computer-generated sleazeball carry out whatever plan he had concocted in his sick electronic brain.

"So whose side are you on?" I demanded. "Victor's? Or mine?"

Paige sighed.

"I have to think it over," she said.

CHAPTER 12

The Agony of Delete

"Mom, I feel sick," I said, as soon as I woke up on Thursday morning. "Can I stay home from school today?"

I didn't really feel sick. I just wanted to make sure I was home all day. The president's State of the Union address was scheduled to be televised at eight o'clock, East Coast time. That would give Victor all day to climb into the computer, transmit himself to Washington, and do whatever he planned to do there.

"Let me feel your forehead."

Mom said she didn't think I had a fever, but she got a thermometer anyway. When she came to take it out of my mouth, the mercury was up to 115 degrees.

"See?" I said. "I'm burning up. I think I should stay home from school."

"Yip, if your temperature was really one hundred fifteen you'd be dead. I know you held the thermometer up to a lightbulb. I'm not going to fall for that old trick again. Get up and get dressed."

"Aw, Mom!" I complained. "I feel awful. What if I pass out in the middle of science class?"

"They'll use you to calculate the speed of falling bodies," she said. "Or maybe they'll dissect you. Get dressed, Yip. I have to go to work."

"Grandpa will be here," I volunteered. "He can take care of me."

"Go to school!"

I watched the clock all day at school. It might as well have been going *backward*. When three o'clock finally arrived, I was out the door before the bell stopped ringing. I threw my leg over my bike and pedaled home like I was in the Olympics, hoping and praying that Victor hadn't gotten there first.

A half a block from our house, I saw somebody climbing the front steps.

"Victor!" I shouted. "Wait!"

He turned and watched me as I skidded up to the steps.

"Remember you said you'd take me through the screen and show me cyberspace?" I said, catching my breath. "Well, I want to go now."

"Tomorrow, okay, Yip?" Victor said hurriedly. "I have important things I need to accomplish today."

"Tomorrow's too late."

"Too bad, Yip."

"I created you, you know," I said, climbing the steps. "You said you owe your existence to me. You promised."

"So what?" Victor asked.

"Friends keep their promises."

"You don't get it, do you?" Victor shouted at me. "When are you going to learn? I am not your friend, Yip! I never was your friend."

My plan wasn't going to work. He wasn't going to take me through the screen with him. There was no backup plan. I didn't know what to do. I couldn't let him get at the computer.

"If you're not my friend, I don't want you in my house anymore," I said, blocking his path. Victor laughed and shoved me out of the way. He reached into his pocket and pulled out a key.

"You open that door and it's trespassing!" I warned him.

"Paige gave me a key," Victor said. "She told me I could come over anytime."

He opened the door and went inside. I followed him.

There were three smeary red footprints in the hallway. We followed them through the living room. There was an arm on the floor sticking out of the kitchen. Victor rushed over.

It was Grandpa Leo, lying on his back. Blood was all over him and all over the floor around him. There was a meat cleaver sticking out of his chest. Grandpa's eyes were closed. His mouth was open.

"Mr. Turner!" Victor exclaimed, rushing to Grandpa's side.

"Very funny, Grandpa," I said. "You can get up now."

"Yip, your grandfather is hurt!" Victor scolded me. "He could die!"

I just rolled my eyes. Grandpa Leo let out a groan. What a ham!

"Need . . . help," Grandpa whispered to Victor.

"I will get you help, Mr. Turner!"

"Ambulance," he whispered. "Call nine-one-one."

Victor grabbed the telephone off the wall.

At that moment, Paige came running in the front door.

"Yip!" she yelled. "I skipped the yearbook meeting!"

Victor touched the "9" key on the phone. When he did, a big yellow spark shot out of the receiver and brushed against his ear.

"Yip—"

There was a loud pop, like the sound of a blown

lightbulb. A hail of sparks shot out of Victor's ear.

"Yipyipyipyipyipyipyipyipyipyipyipyipyipyip."

Then, nothing. Smoke curled out of Victor's ear. He stopped moving entirely. He just stood there, frozen, holding the phone in his hand, like a mannequin in a department store.

"I knew it!" Grandpa leaped off the floor and shouted triumphantly. "He was fake!"

"You did that on purpose, Grandpa?" I asked.

"I rewired the phone," he explained. "I rigged it up to shoot a few hundred volts out the earpiece when the '9' key was pressed."

Paige screamed, then fell to her knees.

"He's dead!" she sobbed.

"Not dead," I corrected her. "Deleted."

"I loved him!" Paige said through her tears. "He's the first boy I ever really loved!"

"You'll find another boy," Grandpa said, carefully hugging Paige so the meat cleaver wouldn't jab her. "A real boy."

"Real boys are jerks," Paige sobbed.

"Not all of them, honey."

Suddenly, Victor's head moved about an inch to the left. Paige, Grandpa, and I looked at him.

"*Pain in arm*," Victor said in a robotic computer

voice. *"Doctor asked if I ever had that pain before. I said yes. Doctor said, 'Well you've got it again.'"*

"What the—" said Grandpa.

"Pain in foot," Victor droned. *"Doctor said he'd have me walking in an hour. He did. He stole my car."*

"He's hallucinating!" Paige exclaimed.

"No, he's not!" I said. "The electrical surge must have wiped out everything in his database except for *The Best of Henny Youngman!*"

Victor started droning on and on:

"My uncle was so bowlegged, when he sat around the house, he sat around the house. . . . A bum asked me for money and said he hadn't tasted food in a week. I told him it still tastes the same. . . . I live so far out of town, the mailman mails me my letters. . . . The doctor gave me six months to live. I didn't pay his bill, so he gave me another six months. . . . The plastic surgeon said he couldn't give my wife a face-lift, so he lowered her body. . . ."

"He must be in pain!" Paige exclaimed. "We have to put him out of his misery."

"His misery?" moaned Grandpa. "We should put him out of *our* misery. I can't stand Henny Youngman!"

Grandpa started fussing with some electrical equipment so he could give Victor a second zap.

"I have another idea, Grandpa," I said. "I don't know why I didn't think of it earlier."

I grabbed the biggest pot in the kitchen, the one Mom uses to boil spaghetti. I brought it over to the sink and turned the faucets on full blast. Once there were a few gallons in there, the pot was really heavy. Paige helped me lift it out of the sink and carry it over to where Victor was standing, still motionless with the phone in his hand.

"*I've been married for thirty-four years and I'm still in love with the same woman,*" Victor droned. "*If my wife ever finds out she'll kill me . . . kill me . . . kill me . . . kill me . . .*"

Paige and I swung the pot back and then swung it forward. The water flew out and hit Victor flush in the face.

The explosion knocked us backward. Victor's whole body shattered into a million pieces, a million tiny fireballs of sparks that were so bright we had to shield our eyes. The sparks flew in all directions, showering the kitchen and then disappearing, like Fourth of July fireworks that disintegrate into nothing before they reach the ground.

The phone dropped to the floor.

There was nothing left of Victor. He was deleted.

"What a world," Grandpa said, shaking his head. "What a world."

The three of us stood there for a minute or two. We were all too stunned to speak. The only sound was the telephone receiver bouncing gently against the wall.

The quiet wasn't broken until we heard sirens coming up the street. Then Mrs. Harrison from next door burst into the kitchen.

"Leo!" she screamed. "Are you all right? I saw an explosion! Your phone line was out."

"I'm fine, Liddy," Grandpa told her. "We . . . spilled a little water."

A bunch of firemen stormed through the door carrying axes and fire extinguishers and all kinds of other equipment.

"Everything's fine, fellows," Grandpa Leo said. "You're not needed here."

"Mister, do you know you've got a meat cleaver sticking out of your chest?" one of the firemen asked Grandpa Leo.

Grandpa showed them how he had stuck the cleaver to a block of wood and strapped the block to his body.

Suddenly, Mom and Dad came rushing in.

"We got here as fast as we could!" Dad said. "They

told us there was an explosion. What's going on?"

"The old man here was playing some sort of prank on the kids and this lady called nine-one-one," one of the firemen explained.

"Pop, I told you not to fool with knives and explosives!" scolded Dad.

"Okay! Okay! I'm sorry!" Grandpa said.

"While we were wasting our time here," one of the firemen lectured Grandpa, "there could have been a *real* emergency somewhere."

"This *was* a real emergency," I said under my breath.

CHAPTER 13

A Valuable Lesson

It took about an hour to explain the true story about Victor to Mom and Dad. Paige and I were afraid Dad was going to punish us, but he didn't. I guess he was just relieved that nobody was hurt. His movie was finally finished and he was happy we could be together again as a family.

After dinner, Dad went down the basement to check out the Synthespian software for himself. Mom went into the kitchen to clean up. Grandpa Leo was in the living room with Paige and me. It was hard to get Victor out of our minds.

"Grandpa," I asked. "How did you know he was computer-generated?"

Grandpa got up and started pacing the floor, the way Sherlock Holmes always did when he explained how he knew who the murderer was.

"As soon as you introduced me to Victor," Grandpa said, "I was suspicious. There was something strange about him. Yesterday I finally figured out what it was—he was too perfect. He didn't bite his nails. He didn't pick his nose. He never stumbled over his words. He didn't seem to have any bad habits."

"So?" I asked.

"No human is that perfect. It occurred to me that it's *flaws* that make an individual human, not perfection. That's when I began to suspect he might have been created with that computer program your dad was telling us about."

"Very clever, Grandpa," Paige said.

"So I did a little detective work," Grandpa continued. "I called Peoria, Illinois, and they had no record of anyone named Victor Turing ever living there. But I thought I remembered hearing the name Turing somewhere, so I went to the library and looked it up."

"And?"

"Alan Turing was a mathematician who helped develop one of the first computers in the 1940s. He spent a good part of his life trying to determine if computers could possess intelligence. That *really* made me suspicious about Victor."

"So he named himself in honor of Alan Turing!" Paige said. "Grandpa, you're a genius!"

"But there was one thing that clinched it for me," Grandpa said. "Victor would never touch your mother's chocolate chip cookies. Anyone who can resist your mother's cookies couldn't possibly be human."

Just thinking about Mom's chocolate chip cookies made me hungry. I could almost smell them.

"Cookies!" Mom shouted from the kitchen. "Come and get 'em while they're hot!"

The three of us raced into the kitchen. As we gobbled the cookies down, Grandpa rewired the telephone so it would work normally again.

"I knew computers were vulnerable to electrical power surges," he said, "so I figured maybe Victor would be, too. I rigged this baby up to deliver a nice jolt. If Victor was human, he would have gotten a shock. He wasn't, so he got his butt zapped back to . . . wherever he came from."

"Cyberspace," I said.

"Well," Paige sighed after wiping off her milk mustache. "I guess I learned *my* lesson."

"Nobody's perfect, right, honey?" Mom asked, hugging her.

"Nah!" Paige giggled. "I learned that you should always make a backup copy of any important data. If I'd done that, when one Victor got zapped, I'd still have another Victor as a spare."

"That's all we would have needed," I groaned. "*Two* Victors."

CHAPTER 14

A Fella Can Change His Mind

A week passed since we had deleted Victor, and I hadn't touched the computer once. Just looking at it made me think how close I had come to causing a national catastrophe.

I was puttering around the house looking for something to do after school. I didn't feel like working on my homework yet. There was nothing good on TV. Paige was with her friends. Dad was at work and Mom was out. I looked around for Grandpa, and finally found him fooling around at the workbench in the garage.

"Hey, Grandpa," I said. "Want to play some football?"

"You mean at your computer?"

"Nah," I said. "At the playground. You want to have a catch?"

"I thought you said you couldn't throw a football."

"Maybe you can teach me."

"Sure!" he said excitedly. "You know, I've been thinking, maybe you can teach me something, too."

"Me, teach *you*?" I asked. "What could I possibly teach you?"

Grandpa motioned for me to follow him. He went into the house and led me downstairs into the basement. Then he sat in the chair in front of the computer. He pulled up another chair next to it and patted it for me to sit down.

"Where's the ON/OFF switch for this thing?" Grandpa asked.

"*You* want to learn how to work the computer?" I said, genuinely shocked. "You hate computers! You said you'd never touch one."

"A fella can change his mind, can't he?" he said. "I've been thinking. If you could take a bunch of electrons and make them into this supposedly perfect boy, well, maybe we could take another bunch of electrons and make them into . . . a perfect old lady."

"A perfect old lady?" I asked.

"Y'know," Grandpa said sheepishly. "Sort of a virtual girlfriend."

"Grandpa! I thought you said Grandma was the only girl for you."

"She was," Grandpa said, smiling at the memory of my grandmother. "But if I can't have reality, I suppose virtual reality just might be the next best thing."

I flipped the switch and the computer jumped to life.